Elaytay (Tay)'s Adventure

In

Space & Time

Part Three

Which Time May Be

by

Lauresa Tomlinson

Young of Heart Publishing
Copyright 2020
Lauresa Tomlinson
Mckinleyville, CA

Dedication

Part Three of Elaytay (Tay)'s Adventures is dedicated to those who like time travel. And to those who have had dreams of different times or realms that seem real.

Author's notes

Started planning part three of Elaytay (Tay) in 2001 and knew what I wanted in it. But it took till Feb 3, 2016 before I finally made all of the notes and ideas into words.

Meanwhile I had been working on 5 other books.

Table of Contents

Elaytay (Tay)'s Adventures in Space and Time

Which Times May be

Verify Time and Space

I have only been back home for a short time, and I was already formulating questions about the new Science of Time Travel.

The idea excited me, and there were so many places I wanted to check out.

Then the big questions came, 'How many lifetimes of information can one gather?

Will we be experiencing time at a faster rhythm than our lives here on our planet?

I mean I wonder if I will experience a few sestrons (days), mistrons (months) or sectos (years) in say a decon (hour) of our own time.

Surely we wouldn't have to spend the same amount of time, because that would take us away from our own lives here.'

Looking at my timelink, "Oh my, if I don't hurry I will be late meeting up with Enah 2(E 2)!" I shouted on my way down the stairs.

Strong Bow met me on the main floor.

"Then you had better hurry, Love," he said reaching out to give me a kiss and a huge hug.

"Be safe and hurry home, but have fun this sestron (day)."he added.

My excitement gained momentum as I headed for the Science Center.

This sestron (day) was the first sestron (day) back at the center, and I would be learning the time travel program we now had on our planet.

'I wondered if I could go back in time and manage to save a crew member from our crash on Earth or at least manage to save DNA samples, so they could be cloned.

But I don't think they would be the same because they would only have memories and not the joys and traumas that go with those memories, so I think that would make them different. But maybe I could yell a warning earlier than I did.'

"Good sestron (day)" I said as I opened the large doors, of the science center. I was greeted by Enah 2 (E 2).

Some things seem to never change.

Enah 2(E 2) was still dressing the same as Master Enasto did when he was alive, with the shoulder length hair and the long green vestment.

It was like having an old friend back except for one thing, Enah 2 (E 2) wasn't programed to limp.

"Come on in. I have a lot to show you," he said motioning for me to follow him.

I followed him as he showed me machines with two touch screens, and holographic dials, levers and buttons on each panel. Then he opened the door to what he called the time chamber. It looked like a large dome from the inside.

"So tell me how does it all work?" I asked trying to hold back my excitement.

"You see that chair in the center of the room?" he asked, pointing to a chair that looked comfortable enough, except for all of the wires hanging above it.

The wires hooked to what looked to be a very strange helmet.

"Yes," I replied, quickly while looking at it a little closer.

The other ends of the wires were attached to panels, with even more dials, switches, slides, touch screens and buttons.

There were a few more screens with visuals and audio trackers on the next panel.

"It's a little complicated," Enah 2 (E 2) started to explain. "We had a little outside help," he continued.

"Outside help?" I questioned.

"Yes, while you were on your first mission to Earth, we learned a lot about the mind, brain, consciousness, spirit and dimensions," he explained.

"So you were learning and working on this from the time I left on my first mission?" I asked clarifying.

"Yes, that is about the time we built our own Creation Domes, and that helps in speeding up our experiments.

With them we are able to make advances by leaps and bounds.

We are now able to see and hear what you see and hear. They also translate the languages so we can understand what is being said," he explained with a slight smile.

"So this is the same type of domes as on Palids?" I questioned.

"Yes, but there have been advances. In this model we can regulate the time. We can keep the same time as the rest of our planet, let time go faster or slow it down to see how some of the fastest moving things in creation actually work.

We have also found that everything created, is connected, - not only in this space and time, but all of them," he said, giving the gesture to everything in sight.

"When you say everything created do you mean everything, including things like these machines, buildings, and all," I said, figuring to rule out a few things.

"Everything that has life and that is naturally made by The Creator's Creative Force and nature," he explained.

"We have done some experimenting

while you were off planet and talked to a lot of what others call wise and holy persons.

They pretty much explained it like this," he continued.

"Quote - "Time is continuous and so the past, present and future are only relevant to the perception of the perceiver. Unquote," he related to me.

"What?" I asked before really thinking about what he said.

"Some of our scientist made this machine to help us mentally be conscious and to be aware of other time lines," he continued while looking at me from over one of the machine.

"I think I am on the same page as you," I said, "Are you talking about living on different time lines or different dimensions, at the same time as we are here? Because Papa Two Wolves said it was important to be mindful here but remain aware of other realms and the lessons they teach." I questioned, just to make sure we were talking about the same thing.

"Yes, in a way I am talking about both. We did find out that we can gather experience from other parts of ourselves and history, and I say _we_ loosely, being a sintho (android)," he said with a smile.

"Okay, now that was a little confusing. Are you talking about learning from other realms?" I said looking at Enah 2 (E 2) across the top of the machine in front of me.

"Yes, let me try to explain it this way. We have found out through experiments that self-aware beings are multi-dimensional creatures, and are like a perfectly cut diamond. We have and do exist on many different levels, worlds, dimensions, time periods, realities, or whatever term you want to use. We are constantly gathering information. All of these areas are held together, by what most are calling Spirit. Some call that part energy, while others call it life force. Haven't you ever been in a situation, needed a solution, and all of a sudden you knew just what to do to help? And you afterwards thinking about the situation had no idea how you knew what to do or where that information came from?" he said pausing.

"Yes," I agreed. 'I'm sure that is what Papa Two Wolves was saying.'

"We are constantly gathering information when we can make that connection to our other parts. For some people making that connection is easier than for others," he explained.

"Okay, so what do these machines have to do with all of that?' I asked.

"We have found that each area has its own vibration. By using varied vibrations, we can pretty much pinpoint the area and time period we want to study more. By finding your core vibration we put that into the machine, and then tell it where and when to place you.

Sometimes you will be going consciously, and at other times it will seem physical, all while being hooked up to this wired helmet through the machine. Your focus will be in that area of time, space, dimension or history. Do you understand so far?" he asked.

"I am pretty sure, but I still have a few questions. When I get through with these trips, will I remember all that I have seen or done? And how long will each trip take?" I questioned, "And will they be mental, conscious, physical, spirit trips or just dream like?"

"That all depends on how well the trip goes. Yes, you will remember all that you see, hear, and do. As to how long you will be on the machine will depend on the area you are in some information will come easily, but I do have to tell you, that time flows differently in other realities, so you may be on the machine for only two decons (hours) and live a mistron (month) in that area. I do want to let you know that you can hear me whispering in one ear, and I can hear everything you say out loud. So there is sort of a two way communication going on the whole time you are hooked to the machine.

Sometimes you may be seemingly in your own body, and at other times you will be invisible to everyone there and only be there as an observer.

So always try to find an area of

reflection when you first get to the other area.

No reflection means you are there as an observer and not able to change anything or inner act," he explained.

"Oh, and I almost forgot, most of the time we will be able to see what you see on this screen, when you are there in first person.

As an observer what we see may be a little foggy, so you may have to explain to us what is happening at times," he added pointing to a larger screen off to one side.

"Do we have any holographs of past trips?" I asked.

"Yes, I have a few short ones with me. Would you like to see them?" Enah 2 (E 2) asked while pointing toward a cabinet in a side wall.

"Yes, please.

"Maybe that will give me even a better idea of what we are talking about. I'm pretty sure I understand now, but this will make me feel even more secure in what we are doing," I replied.

"So can you see what I am seeing in the areas I will be exploring or watching?" I added.

"In a way we can make out a few things. Here let me show you what I mean," he said as he turned on the Holiguard (holographic screen).

"This is the recorded brainwave activity of a person who wasn't visible – and visited as an observer. Our machines have been programed to translate brain patterns as close as possible, and we will do a few pattern tests on you after you are hooked up.

This way we can better match your patterns to objects and feelings," he explained.

"And the few test runs that we do can verify the accuracy," he added.

"That sounds good. How accurate do you think these visuals were with what really happened to this person?" I asked.

"I am glad to say we have it down to a 97.998percent chance that what is happening is being seen on our screens," he said reassuring me.

"So when you say during the testing, something you can verify, do you mean something around here that you know very well?" I asked.

"Yes, that is right. You will be shown patterns, pictures and listening to a group of sounds, this will help to start out. Then we can fine tune the machine as close as we can with an actual trip, if needed," he explained.

"Good, let's get started," I said.

"Maybe you should eat first, the testing may take a while," he suggested with a smile

"Yes, that does sound good." I agreed quickly.

"Can you be back in about thirty keptrons (minutes)?" Enah 2 (E 2) asked looking over his shoulder at me.   .

"Yes, I am sure of it. See you in a little

while," I said while walking through the large oversized doors.

As I ate my sandwich, I was trying to think of a place to visit on my first trip.

'Maybe I could just revisit the time Kerzna (Kern) the Watapaw came to live with us. After all, Enah 2 (E 2) has visited us many times and has gotten to know Kerzna (Kern), and he will know if he is seeing things right.'

But in the back of my mind I was wondering, *'If while I'm on a trip as an observer, if I was to whisper a message in the ear of others there -- maybe like a warning, would they be able to get the message? If so then just maybe I could give the warning a little sooner than I did before we crashed. But then if I did and it was able to save the life of even one of my crew, what would that change here.'*

Wow, just thinking about all that made me dizzy.' I finished lunch and got back to the center.

"Ah, I see your back. Good, we can get started," Enah 2 (E 2) said in a cheery voice,

"Come over here and sit down in this chair and lean back. I will be placing the helmet on your head and making sure that all of the connections are in the right places for you.

If you look closer at the helmet you can see that the connections are adjustable in different directions. This is so we can fit it to other planetary travelers who want to help explore history and other places," he continued.

"Good, I am glad to know that it will be

fitted to just me, and it's not a generic helmet – one size fits all, because those never work on everyone," I said in laughter.

"I think everything is in place now. Let me turn on a few things over here, and we will start out verifying what you are seeing and hearing before we let you go on your first time mission," he said while pushing a few buttons and adjusting a few knobs to set things up.

"Ah, there you are. I see the leaves across the way caught your eye, and you're able to hear the hum from the electronics in the next room. That is very good. It looks like you may just be one of our best travelers yet," he said sounding very confident.

I looked over at the viewing screen that he had just turned, so I could see it.

"Wow! I'm not seeing leaves. I'm seeing me looking at me infinity in a screen," I heard myself almost shout in excitement.

Enah 2 (E 2) chuckled, "Yes you are seeing you looking at the screen repeatedly because you were looking at the screen that recorded you looking at the screen."

Now let me set up the recording, so you can see what we saw when you were looking at different objects, like the leaves," he said handing me a few pictures to look at,

"Look though these while I record the screen."

I looked through the photos a few times then handed them back to him.

"Okay, look at the screen again, and I will play what was recorded while you were look at the photos.

This is what I saw you looking at," he said, flipping a switch.

Sure enough, there were the photos I looked at just the way I remember seeing them, except for the sort of fuzzy edging that seemed to circle the outer edge of the screen.

"We have just a few more adjustments to fine tune before your first trip.

Close your eyes and bring up a memory in great detail," he requested. "Good. Now we can start the other tests, like the ones for the feelings and emotions.

Try to remember one of the most emotional times in your life," he prompted me.

That was easy. I could recall my crash on Earth during my first mission as if it were sacytron (yesterday) and just thinking about losing my best friends brings tears to my eyes.

"Excellent! The emotions came though clearly, and we even got visuals. This is amazing," he said pushing the emotional date down to the lower right hand corner of the holographic screen, and bring up the contrast of the visuals.

"Good work, indeed! I think we are ready for a trial mission."

"So how does this work? Do you send me to a special point, or do I need to think of a place in time or space?" I asked, turning to look at him.

"Oh, no need for you to do anything except just sit and relax.

Our group of scientist and the council has made a list of places and times to investigate and gather info from, he explained.

"Will there be a time when I can travel to a place in time that I pick?" I asked, trying to relax.

"Breathe deep now and relax even more.

I am sure we will work out a time for you to play in time," came the reply in what seemed to be a dream.

Chapter One

The Sphinx and the Under city

I felt as if I was waking from a good long nap. I opened my eyes, and slowly looked around the room.

I wasn't in the Time Chamber any more. So where had Enah 2 (E 2) sent me?

There were vases of gloriously colored flowers all around the room, and the aroma was mildly sweet.

I would say just sweet enough to make the room pleasant and relaxing.

The walls were adorned with jeweled reliefs of beautiful scenes of wildlife and peoples working together.

It all seemed familiar somehow.

A young girl entered the room, and the name Nika (Nicky) sprung to mind, and she seemed to be my handmaiden.

"Good morning my queen, I brought your attire for the days meetings, and here is your basin of fresh water," she said

I seemed to know her even though I never remembered meeting her.

She is a very lovely young girl, with black shoulder length hair, green eyes, and slender built,

I would guess she may be in her early twenties.

I'm now standing at the basin of water, and I can see my reflection in it as I was instructed, so that means I am really here.

I have long black hair, and large green eyes, and my skin is almost a light beige in color.

I seem to be a little over six feet.

"What is planned for today?" I asked while she helped me get dressed.

"You are to meet with Molnan (Mole), and talk over the order of inspections," she said with a bow as she went to the door, and motioned for someone in the hallway to enter.

A tall man with light bronze skin entered the room, and bowed deeply,

"Jewavaneef (Neef), My Queen I have your schedule for the day.

If it pleases you, I will go over it with you now," he said.

"Yes, Molnan (Mole), come sit, and tell me what is planned," I said, taking a closer look at him as he grew near.

His dark hair lay in deep waves, and was tied behind his head.

His green eyes sparkled as emeralds

against his golden brown skin.

He opened the scrolls as he sat down near me.

"Today is the day you inspect the Sphinx and name it as the Under City's official protective entrance.

I have logged all of the extra sensor locks, and their locations.

I also have all of the drawings that you have given to me in the past.

I would like to go over them, and mark the order you want to do the inspection in. If that meets with your approval, My Queen," he said.

"Yes I agree, that will give me a chance to see if there are any other changes I would like to see made," I said, reaching for a few of the scrolls sitting beside him.

As I touch the scrolls, I am flooded with memories. I already know all that is on the scrolls as if I had drawn them myself.

I sprawled the first scroll out on the table before us, and pointed to the very large monument – like building in the center of the first page, the Under City was in a dotted area indication its location underground.

"Yes, this is right. It was to have the face, and head of a female to show wisdom, knowledge, and discernment, and the body of a lion, the symbol of strength.

This was designed to be large enough to be seen by our sister ships from Ephizna (our home planet).

They will be arriving soon to help with the expansion of the Under City.

Last message received said that Ephizna was about to explode.

This Sphinx was designed to show the position of quick action with its front paws out in front ready to leap.

Its left paw holds the entrance to the first area," I said while pointing to its paw.

"This will be my starting point. This is where a person entering will be faced with the first of many choices to make before gaining entrance to the maze that leads to the Under City."

"Yes, it is marked as the first," Molnan (Mole) nodded.

"Mark this as the second point," I said pointing at the xtelift (wall-less elevator) which is activated by harmonics,

"Unless the traveler can sense the right level to stop on, they may end up in a storage vault; this is my second point of inspection.

If the person makes the right choice, then they will come across three healing rooms on the right, one room for the physical, one for mental, and one for emotional, and one room on the left for the communication chief. And that will be my third point of inspection.

From there we will go to the celebration chamber, and my fourth point will be the large vault which will store the special grain to feed the world later when needed.

The storage vault should be in the shape of a pyramid to keep the grain viable for the future.

It is important that all sensors in these areas are working.

Then there is the area that leads to the living maze that leads to the Under City.

This will be my fifth point of inspection" I explained.

"Yes my Queen they are all so noted" answered Molnan (Mole) with a head nod.

"I need to know that all of the sensors can read the thoughts, emotional, and mental states of any person wanting to enter the Under City. The walls of the maze will be ruled by sensors that can tell what is in the heart, and mind of the one wanting to enter the Under City, and if that doesn't ring pure, they will be lost forever in the maze," I informed him.

"Lost forever?" he asked.

"Yes, because the walls of the maze will change, and be different with each person that enters it, and the sensors will be reading all energy and mental thoughts from the person going through the maze. They are to be constantly scanned for any changes," I said.

"If you please, my Queen, I would like to know what happened if more than one person enters at a time, and one of them does not ring pure of heart, and mind?" he pleaded.

"Then the maze will divide the group,

and only let the ones that ring as pure will be allowed entrance into the City. We only want those with the love of nature, thoughtful, and kindness of heart to have sanctuary in the Under City.

It is to remain a place of peace for all. A place of safety for generations to come, when all others become lazy, and have hearts of hatred, and evil thoughts toward others," I explained, while looking over the other scrolls with all of the technical measurements, and instructions for building this great monument,

"All of these scrolls are to be taken into the Under City today."

All who had been working on it knew it needed to last for a very long time.

For there would be many changes the Earth and its inhabitance would go through besides weather, storms, floods, earthquakes, and anything else that might happen, for it was to help keep the special ones, their wisdoms and knowledge safe.

The under City was designed so that it had its own food, water, and power sources.

There are garden areas, and all of the things that one would have above.

They were working on the areas that would seem like the sun was shining.

I could remember seeing a few on my last trip to the Under City.

It was amazing; there was the sun for day, and stars at night, air flow, and even a few trees, and grass areas.

There are plans to expand as needed and that is where our last ships will help in the building of the other levels." I explained.

Molnan (Mole) looked up from the scrolls, "It is time for the inspections, My Queen."

"Of course, you are right. Summon the transport while I finish here," I said, while rolling up the last scroll.

Shortly Nika (Nicky) was at the door, "Transport has arrived, My Queen."

"Thank you, Nika (Nicky), I will be back shortly. Have my meal ready for me," I instructed.

I met Molnan (Mole) at the palace entrance, and boarded the transport.

It was only a few minutes to the Sphinx site.

I gathered all of the Captains, and Chiefs around, and explain to each of them the order of my inspections.

They all walked along with me down the stairs to inspection each point, giving themselves peace of mind that their area was completed.

As we got to the xtelift (wall-less elevator), and it rose to the top, I pointed to the rest of the hallway which lead to the West.

"In that hall on my right is where my burial chambers is, right?" I asked for verification.

"Yes, My Queen, would it please you to see it now?" Molnan (Mole) asked.

"No, I will view it later, right now we have more pressing matters ahead of us," I said with a motion to go forward to the next point.

"I can see all of the healing chambers are properly equipped," I said as I looked through each one,

"And I see that our communication center is on top of things," I said walking down the hall toward the celebration chamber.

"This Chamber is magnificent; the artwork is enough to put anyone in a celebrative mood.

Thanks to all of you, we have something to be proud of. Now next to the last thing on my list is the vault,"

I said turning to leave the celebration hall.

Molnan (Mole) sang the harmonics then blew the whistle to finish the combination, and the vault wall swung open.

"This is beautiful. The pyramid here is large enough to hold a very large pot of the grain.

Now I need to know that the deflector rods, that help to frame, protect and support this pyramid are in place right?

And that no outside sensors can penetrate these walls, and the top of it is in the chest of the sphinx?"

"Yes my queen, just as you designed it,"

Molnan (Mole) answered after looking at one of the captains.

"Please My Queen, I need to ask how large do you want the grain storage pot to be, while I am thinking of it?" Molnan (Mole) asked, "The one that will be housed here in the Sphinx," he clarified as I inspected a few small details in the vault

"Make it very large, as large as you can get.

And make sure it is sealed. It has to feed the world in the future.

I want it to almost fill the cavity of the pyramid inside of the Sphinx," I said, looking over my shoulder at him.

"Yes, My Queen, I will see to it,"

I nodded approval, "Then let's go to the gateway to the Under City."

I don't think that any of them understood that the maze could change.

I had each component of the maze put together by different groups, and they were transported to their portions with the equipment need for each job, so no one group really knew what the last group did.

But when it is turned on, the sensors would run scans of everyone who wanted entry, and change the maze accordingly.

Right now the sensors are turned off, this way I knew I could take the whole group through without having to worry about getting lost.

The three gate keeper in the Under City had control over the sensors, and they could be turned off, and on, as long as all three agreed.

The safety was that their stations were far enough apart that one gate keeper couldn't control any more than the one station he was assigned to.

Each one had different ways of proving it was their station, and the safety proofs were cycled, and they are cycled at a different rate. So the info asked for was only known by the gate keeper for that station.

"I love the work that was done on the entry gate to the maze. It is absolutely impressive." I said turning to the chief that I knew had designed it.

The ability of the maze to change was even a secret to him.

He bowed graciously, and I continued.

"The path to the Under City will be pretty straight because the gate keepers had orders to keep them off till all is ready, and ordered."

As we walked the path, I could hear whispers behind me.

Each group was recognizing the part of the walls they had put in place.

I had to smile, each of them were so proud of their work, little did they know that those very walls they thought were stationary, could move to make a different path.

Stopping, I turned to them, "Something

that I don't think any of you know is that each wall that you put into place can change positions.

Some fully change directions while others pivot in the middle to form a new path to the Under City or to trap the unworthy."

All of them stood there wide eyed, as if stunned for a few seconds then looked at each other.

"This is to keep the Under City a safe haven for all of us, and safe from invaders," I informed them, as they looks around at each other wide eyed.

"Well, I think we have all seen enough to get the idea. It is getting close to your afternoon break, so let's all go back to the surface." I said after a short pause.

Molnan (Mole) received word that the transport was ready and waiting for us.

While in the transported back to the palace, word came through that we were about to be invaded by one of the warring planets in the belt of Orion.

"Give the word to turn the maze on and for everyone to get into the Under City now!

And after I get out I want you to make sure that all of the grain is taken in with you to keep it safe. The storage grain pot can be made later.

I don't want anything left to change. I will meet you there in the great hall,"

I said as I left the transport, "Everything

else is set up. I have a few items to get before I meet you there."

Nika (Nicky) hurried to meet me on the palace steps.

"Nika (Nicky)! Get everyone here to the Under City now!

There is no time to answer questions just do it!" I commanded.

"Yes, right away,' she said running down the hall.

I ran to my room to gather Mulnanx my pet cat.

I looked out the window just in time to watch the last guardian enter the paw of the sphinx as everything went black.

'Something must have happen back in the time chamber.

Maybe they just lost power for a few minutes.

Don't panic, just wait, you'll see, the lights will come back on, and you will be safe in the chamber chair, relax, slow your breathing.

I think I am lying down. Ok go with that feeling, relax.

I'm okay, everything is okay. Enah 2 (E 2) will have everything under control soon.

Think of the Sphinx – yes, the walls are all finished, and decorated, and the harmonic detectors, and sensors are all in place, and turned on by now.

The Under City is well prepared; there is enough power to keep it going for tens of thousands of years.

That's odd I don't hear anything.' Hoping

secretly the invasion was a false report.

'Oh good, I'm standing near the window I can see its light again, and I can see the Sphinx is still standing.

Mulnanx wasn't in my arms anymore.'

"Mulnanx, where are you?

Here nanx, come here baby, where are you?

Oh there you are, what are you doing over there?" I asked while walking around the table,

"Oh! What? That can't be! How is my body laying – but I'm here."

Mulnanx looked up at me, and then back at the body lying on the floor.

He looks as confuse as I felt. Kneeling down I tried to shake my body, but my hand just went through it.

I caught sight of Nika (Nicky) at the door out of the corner of my eye.

Then trying to pet my cat – he let out a strange cry, and jumped back as my hand went through his paw.

Mulnanx went through the door with Nika (Nicky) shadowing him, and I sighed with relief.

'He'll get help, and it will all be okay.'

"Nika (Nicky) must be running for the Doctor!"

She came back in a flash with the Doctor. "Over here Doctor Bulnak (Bull)," motioned Molnan (Mole).

Bulnak felt my neck, and shook his

head, Nika (Nicky) started crying, "How?" she asked.

"I figure it was that large ceiling tile that fell," explained Bulnak.

"It can't be! I'm right here!" I screamed,

"Can't you hear me? Look I'm right here standing in front of you."

'Maybe I can get back in the body.

I can't be dead there is so much I need to do yet.

I am sorry now that I didn't listen in class when they were teaching about death, and the separation.

I have no idea what to expect. No! No!

I'm not dead I refuse to believe that! Not now, we just got things set for a good life here on this planet.

We have no place to go back to, thanks to the Rojentics (Rojects) (a united warrior planet). I don't think I will ever understand them.

Why would you blow up something you want because the people who have it, refuse to give it to you?

It seems there is always a chance to change things as long as there is a future.

But the Rojentics (Rojects) are living proof there are hot heads in creation, I guess.

But why today, of all days?

Well maybe I can stick around long enough to see my burial chambers.

Wonder if there is still a way to get things done without talking to any of them.'

I thought while trying to pick up the

papers on my desk.

'Nope, my hand went right through them and my desk. So now what do I do? I have no body.'

Two of my guards came into the room, and Doctor Bulnak (Bull) instructed them to take my body, but I didn't hear where. I was too lost in my own thoughts.

"Wait! Where are you taking me?"

'Since you can't see or hear me, it won't hurt to follow you.

Hum, if I'm dead then of course they have to get my body ready for burial.'

Everything was done quickly;

I overheard one of the technicians saying there may be another attack wave coming at any time.

Soon everyone of importance was gathered for the burial march. Molnan (Mole) came with both arms very full of scrolls, and books.

When we got close to my tomb's door Molnan (Mole) handed all of the scrolls and books to one of the others near him, and he held up both hands, and sang the harmonics then on the last note pushed on the two stones at the same time.

The door gave up the sound of air moving then pivoted in the center.

I could see into the vault from either side of the door, and Molnan (Mole) did make sure that the walls were decorated with the histories pasts, and futures as I had related them to him.

'Excellent job Molnan (Mole) I just wish I could thank you properly.

Molnan (Mole) took the scrolls back and place them in a holding chamber under my sarcophagus.

These were my life histories and my discoveries.

The stone lid was slid back into place to seal the scrolls and I, that is, my body was placed inside.

"Well good bye body. Now what?"

'I should have studied more about this kind of thing. Maybe it's time to explore.'

They are closing, and locking my tomb.

'Guess it is time, though there were so many things I wanted to do. "Oh!Fraznut!" 'I'm hearing a whooshing sound.

What is that? It's getting louder, and closer.' "AAAAAH! 'I'm in the dark again.

What the…? Oh I'm in space, I can see the stars now, and there is Earth.

I'm just floating out here? Is this what after life is all about?

If it is then I feel cheated.

I started moving my arms and legs trying to turn and see all around me. I think I have figured out how to move around out here. It's sort of like swimming.

If I move my arms in the direction I want to go, and put bother feet together then I move in that direction, and move my feet apart I slow to a stop. I'm drifting higher, but I want to go back to the planet.'

"Wait! No fair!" *'I keep going the wrong direction; nothing is working like it did a few minutes ago.'*

"Hey, can anyone hear me? Is there anyone out here but me?"

'I'm getting farther, and farther out into space.'

"HELLO?"

'Well I guess floating in space is where it's at. Might as well relax.

I didn't know there was this many starts out here, they don't all show up on the ship's view screen.

Come to think about it, isn't about time I should be called back to the Time Chamber?

No one said anything about going through death on these trips.'

"Enah 2 (E 2)? Can you hear me? Ouch!"

'Tapping what should be the helmet in the times chamber just hurt my ears.'

"Hurt? Guess I'm not as dead as I thought if that hurt. Are you supposed to feel pain if you're dead?" I said aloud, I can hear my voice.

Gee I wish I would have listened in class."

"Feel?" said a voice from behind me. I spun around to find out who was talking.

All I seen was a flash of very bright light.

"Who are you?" I meant to find out all I could in the shortest amount of time.

"I'm Elzoid (Zod), I help all who enter this realm," said this seemingly white cloaked entity, now floating near me in space.

"And, just what realm is this may I ask?"

"It's a holding realm. You won't be here long enough that it will make much of a difference," came the voice clearly,

"You're just between stops, sort of."

"Sort of?" I questioned.

A cough jolted me, and I felt my helmet fall off.

Seeing sparks made me blinked, I'm back in the time chamber.

"What the?" Things are in such a mess.

There are wires hanging loose all over, and some are live.

Some of the machines are tipped completely over, and some are leaning on others. I managed to get to my feet.

"Wow!" *Better take it a little slower – that was a freebee.*

My head was still spinning but I caught site of Enah 2 (E 2) sprawled out on the floor behind one of the consoles.

Moving a chair, and some wires I managed to get to him. I did a quick check.

'There were no broken areas and no sparks so I think it will be ok to push on his back just right of where the 3rd lumbar would be…. He once told me there was a reset on his back in a special protected area, and if I was lucky I just may have pushed the right spot.'

"Oh! Thank you Elaytay (Tay), I'm glad you got back ok," he said after a few blinks.

"What happened here?" I asked.

"There was a large quake, and it shook for a long time then bounced everything very high, and I guess I got hit by something. Next thing I know you are here, and I'm resetting everything." He answered slowly.

"Just think, if it hadn't been for that last high bounce, I may have had to float in space for a while," I said,

"We need to have safeties added to these programs so if something like this happen again or if there is no one around to bring me back – it will go into auto, and bring me back if I do something strange, like tap my ears."

"What happened? The last part I remember you were being invaded."

"Well I got killed in the process, and then floated around in space for a while, till I coughed, and the helmet fell off.

I am thinking that the big bounce you talked about helped with the helmet coming off," I explained

"Hello! Anyone in there?" came a voice from the other side of the main doors.

"Yes, Elaytay (Tay), and I are blocked in with live wires dancing on some of the equipment. Can you cut the power?" Enah 2 (E 2) explained.

"Yes! Yes, right away. Just hold tight and I will be back with help. Do either of you need a doctor?"

"No, just minor scratches is all," answered Enah 2 (E 2).

"I wonder how much of the trip was recorded," I asked.

"I have no idea at this point, and I don't want to try, and run the console till we know it's not going to blow up or catch fire. And I don't want to take a chance of losing what we did manage to record," he explained.

"Okay, I am back with help, and the power is shut off. We will have you out of there very soon," came the voice, from the other side of the door.

"We will do what we can from this side," Enah 2 (E 2) told them.

We untangled wires, and moved file cabinets, consoles and boxes for about half of a decon (hour), and finally the doors opened.

Strong Bow was one of the people helping to get us out.

He grabbed me, and gave me a big hug right off. "I am so glad you are alright, he said giving me another hug. Do you need my help anymore?" He turned to ask the main leader of the rescue team, "If not I would like to take this one home."

"No, go right ahead, most of what we have to do here is clean up, and logging the equipment, and listing what needs to be replaced," came the answer.

"If you need my help you know how to

get hold of me," Strong Bow told them.

They nodded, and we left.

We walked through the large doors into what was left of the sunlight.

The purple skies were starting to turn to the bluer side of the color scale. And I felt good about the time trip except for the last part.

Walking along the path on the way home holding hands with my love, I soon found myself humming the song Nika (Nicky) had been singing as she first entered my chambers.

"Hello Mom, Dad," Elmosa (Mosa) shouted as we got closer to the front gate.

"Hello, how bad was the quake here at the house?" I asked.

Grams came out of the house about that time.

"This old house was made back when they made things to last, and she did find. Not a problem at all." She said. "How did things go at the time lab today? How bad was it there? Come tell us all about it. Dinner is almost ready," she said as we a entered the house.

"Umm, everything smells so good, and you picked vegetables fresh from the garden today it looks like," I said.

"Thank you, and yes of course. So tell me all about what happened today.

I want to hear all of the details," Grams said, urging me to tell all.

"Soon Grams, soon. I will let everyone

know while we are eating.

It was a great day, except for the last part," I said, taking a plate of mixed vegetables to the table.

While we ate I told them all about what happened at the Science Center, and in the Time Chamber.

"I don't want you going on another trip until all of the safety programs and their backup programs are in place," Strong bow interrupted.

"I totally agree. I told Enah 2 (E 2) this before I left today, but I will still need to go help get things back up and running," I agreed. "So enough about, that tell me what happened here this decon (day)."

"Elmosa (Mosa) has news from Earth," Strong Bow said.

"Oh yeah, so what did you hear? How are things going there?" I asked, feeling anxious.

"Well, Rogna – now known as Soaring Hawk, and Aunt Morning Star are having a baby.

They figure in about two mistrons (months)," Elmosa (Mosa) announced proudly.

"Well it looks like you will get to be a cousin after all," I said, and everyone joined in the laughter.

"Yes, and I can hardly wait," he said excitedly.

"So how bad was the quake here," I

asked looking at gramps.

"Well, hum, let's see," Gramps said, stroking his chin with a chuckle. "It wasn't bad here just scared the bu-gees-us out of the chickens and Kerzna (Kern) wasn't too happy about it.

They don't have quakes on his planet. But all in all I think we did good."

Strong Bow spoke up, "Kerzna (Kern) said, that since all of the children were pretty much grown, that he wants to start a family of his own but wants to stay here, and live with us.

I told him I would talk to all of you tonight, and give him an answer in the kunar (morning)."

"Wow, I think that would be great. But how will he find a mate?" I asked

"I think we will leave that part up to him," Strong Bow said laughing.

"Agreed," said Gramps, "He may have to send for one from his home planet."

"But there may be a mate for him on this planet now since we have gotten so strongly into planetary exchanges," Grams spoke up.

"Either way I will tell him we are ok with his idea," Strong Bow said.

I helped clean up after dinner while the guys went and checked on the wellbeing of the farm.

Then Grams and I sat on the front porch

and I told her a few more details of the trip today.

But it didn't take long for the guys to get back.

When Gramps got to the top step, Grams stood up and grabbed his hand. "We have some planning to do if Kerzna (Kern) plans to raise a family," she said leading him into the house.

That left Strong Bow and me alone on the porch. Elmosa (Mosa) went inside as soon as they got back.

We just sat and enjoyed each other's company for a while and watched the second moon come up.

"What a beautiful night. This time of the evening when the sky turns a deep blue reminds me of Earth," I said.

"I agree this is my favorite time of sestron (day). And I want to keep spending it with you for as long as we can.

That is the reason I don't want you to go on any more times trips until they get <u>ALL</u> of the safety programs in place," he said looking sternly at me, "And I mean ALL!"

"I understand that and I agree. But you do know there is a certain amount of risk doing anything in life.

I do need to go help get things back up and running.

The information I brought back today was very interesting and I need to make sure that it is all saved.

If the recording was taken off line before I got back then I will need to explain to the keepers what happened from that point," I added.

"Just be careful, that is all I ask. I don't want to stand in the way of what makes you happy. I just worry about your safety, because I love you so much," he said.

"I know this and I love you very much for that," I said giving him a kiss.

"Ok, it's getting a little cool. Let's go in and call it a good dresto (night)," he said putting his arms around me.

"Time for bed I think, it may be a long sestron (day) prezino (tomorrow)," I said walking upstairs.

"Sleep Well all," we almost said in unison.

Chapter Two
Time out

Wow, amacron (morning) came early, and the sun was almost completely above the hill just beyond our back yard. Strong Bow was gone, so I figured he and Gramps were out taking care of farm chores like normal. I got dressed and hurried down stairs. Grams was busy in the kitchen.

"Here put these on the table, our guys should be in real soon," she said handing me a large plate of biscuits, "finish setting the table please," she added.

"Where is Elmosa (Mosa)?" I asked.

"He hurried out earlier to help Kerzna (Kern) find the proper placement for his new home. This is the most excited I have seen him in a while," she said laughing.

"I can see where this is going to be quite a project, and right up close to the top of Elmosa (Mosa) list," I said with a chuckle.

"Elaytay (Tay), I got to thinking about what happened yesterday and we need to talk before you leave for the science center this sestron (day), Grams said in all seriousness.

OK, it sounds important. How about while we clean up the kitchen," I suggested.

"Yes that will be a good time. I just heard the guys coming up the back stairs. Help me get the rest of this on the table," she said grabbing a few more plates of food.

Strong Bow came through the door first and gave me a big hug and a kiss. Gramps came through next and gave Grams a big hug lifting her off her feet a few lanfases (inches) and they laughed as he put her down.

"Breakfast smells great," Elmosa (Mosa) announced as he came in running through to get washed up.

"Elmosa (Mosa) has the right idea, both of you get washed so we can eat while it's warm," Grams said laughing while gesturing with her hands toward the bathroom.

After everyone was back at the table and grace had been said, it was time to catch up with what was happening on the farm.

"So who has something new that happened since sun up?" grams asked looking around the table at everyone.

"Well Kerzna (Kern) is still figuring out where he wants to put his house. He was thinking, by the barn where the land starts to rise," Elmosa (Mosa) said.

"That would be fine, but remind him that he will need to make a burrier on the higher side on his house to keep out the water that runs off the hill in the wet season," Gramps chimed in.

"What else is happening on the farm?" asked Grams looking around the table.

"Nothing really new, Ol'Doc (neighbor)'s bulica broke down the fence again to get to our females. I told him the last time I wasn't giving him any more of their off spring if it was to happen again," gramps said with a chuckle, "It took a while to get the fence back in place, but it's up now and I will be stringing charging beams across the top."

"Good that sounds like a great plan," Grams said with a chuckle.

"When did you have planned to go to the science center today?" Strong Bow asked looking at me.

"I figured I would hang out here at the house till after lunch, making it a short day," I answered with a smile.

"Good I will get to see you for lunch then. We have a few more things that need to get finished before lunch," he said, while getting up and putting his plate in the sink.

"This is true, we have to hang the charged wire and do a few other things before lunch," Gramps said, taking one last bite.

Elmosa (Mosa) was sitting there is deep thought, taking a bite every once in a while.

"What are you thinking about so intently?" I asked looking for a response.

"Just thinking about Kerzna (Kern)'s house, and the type of barriers would be needed if he builds his house half way up the hill," he said taking another bite.

"Explain," I said.

"Well, if we were to raise the land, making a mound between his house and the hill crest, the water may splash over into his house and if we were to dig a trench the water may still spill over into his house," he said looking puzzled.

"Sounds like you've been giving it a little thought. Ask Gramps and your dad what they think and then ask them if a natural barrier would work in this case to redirect the water flow," I suggested.

"Good thought mom, I was just thinking of asking dad and Gramps before starting the project," he said while putting his plate in the sink.

"Hold on, not so fast. Take these out to Kerzna (Kern), I imagine he is hungry too," Grams said handing Elmosa (Mosa) a basket of fruit.

"Okay," he said grabbing it as he ran out the door.

It didn't take long for Grams and me to get the kitchen clean and ready for lunch. This gave us plenty of time to work on projects while sitting on the porch and talking.

"What you said yesterday when you got back home about spending pretty much a day dealing with what you called the sphinx reminded me of things that have happened to me. I don't know if it was a vision or a dream, but I would often find myself in a different life, for the lack of a better way of putting it. Anyway, I would be in a different life and completing a project which seemed to take the better part of a day, but when I got back here only a decon (hour) had gone by. I talked to a few of our wiser peoples and they said it was just a shift in consciousness. This happens once in a while when we are a wake because we are actually living on many planes at the same time. But most of the time we travel like this while our bodies are asleep and that if we travel during the waking state it is usually because something needs to be corrected or fixed as soon as possible. Does that make sense to you?" she asked, while looking out into the yard from her mending.

"Yes, I think you are right, and I have had short trips most of my life but hadn't really thought too much about it till now. That must be where we get our problem solving skills from," I said laughing.

"I remember once, when it turned out a little more real than I thought. In the area I was traveling there were a lot of brier bushes and I got stuck pretty hard a few times, but finished the mission and got back here. But when I woke up, there was blood on my sleeve where the brier bush had stuck into my arm. I guess that is about as real as it gets. When you are traveling in the time chamber please keep that in mind. So please be very careful" she said looking straight at me, "I think that is what the time chamber is doing but using electronics to put you in a special area of time and space." She explained, "But know this normally you are connected to all these areas and the one you leave from serves as anchor point. It's sort of like leaving the light on in the window so you can find your way back, and even if the helmet didn't fall off, I am sure you would have gotten back. It may have taken a little longer because you were sent to that area artificially and didn't establish the path yourself." She continued.

"I totally agree. When I was there inspecting the Sphinx it felt totally real," I said.

"That is because it was real. But because you didn't go there though your normal channels, when the machines went off line, you were lost for a while. I am just glad that your helmet fell off otherwise you may still be floating in the neither realm," she said. "Now you see why it is so important for the machines to have safety programs in place with an auxiliary backup to help shift you back to this time and space. I did a lot of studies on this when I was younger and always thought it fascinating," she continued.

"That explains a lot of things I have experienced in the past," I said feeling relieved, "Have you found a good way to get back if you

get shocked out of the area you were visiting?"
I asked.

"Not really, never had formal training, but I was told it could take a while if you were to get jolted from one area to another while traveling. I've been told that if you travel on your own naturally, there is a natural connection between your physical body and your soul or astral body that helps you get back. Some have called it the golden thread. I'm thinking that being shocked or jolted like you were would make you disoriented till you figured out what was happening around you. But in this case when the others send you places, just be real careful and make sure there is a backup plan that doesn't rely on the main power grid," she said looking at me seriously.

"Oh, I promised Strong Bow last night that there would be safety programs in place before I go on the next trip, but I do like the idea of having it hooked to a different power source." I said.

Just then Kerzna (Kern) came bounding up to the porch *'Thank you for the fruit Grams,'* he relayed in thought.

"Your quite welcome, I figured you needed the energy to work on the planning of your house. Have you located a female yet?" Grams answered.

'No, not yet, but my mate will be found by my planet. We have special ways of finding just the

right mates for each of us,' he related.

"That sound nice, there a many cultures that help in picking the mated pairs," Grams said.

"What have you heard from Notnah (Not)?" he asked.

"I heard from him yesterday. He is taking classes at the Space Academy and has a room there with two other cadets." Gram said aloud.

He bowed and took off running to the hill where Elmosa (Mosa) was waiting.

"You know, come to think about it, when Kerzna (Kern) came to live with us, I don't think he was much older than Elmosa (Mosa). There may be as much as five to eight sectos (years) between them," Grams said with a chuckle.

"I think you right, and that may be the reason they always got along as well as they do. Kerzna (Kern) is like the brother he never had," I said joining in the laughter.

"Well that's enough sitting, time to get our chores done before lunch," Grams said while getting up and heading for the door.

"True, I'm right behind you," I chimed in.

Grams had a schedule for things to get done so that everything on the farm would run smooth. Everything had its place and needed to be in that space if it wasn't being used at that time. This is the way she raised me and I hadn't thought of life any other way. I never had to hunt for the things I needed because there they always where they belonged.

Morning went fast and lunch time was here. I hurried downstairs to help with lunch.

"Did you get everything done upstairs?" Grams asked as I came through the kitchen door.

"Yes everything is in its place, and all of the beds are made," I announced with a grin, "Plus I got a little reading done."

"Good, you can start on the salad while I work on finishing the main course," she said while humming her favorite song.

Just as I finished putting the salad on the table, Grams turned and said, "Go ring the bell for lunch."

I went to the back door, stepped out onto the back porch and then right back into the house.

Grams looked up and started laughing, "Their stomach bells already rang?"

Grams' laugh is very contagious and I couldn't help but to laugh too, "Yep, must have, cause they are almost racing to the house."

Grams motioned for them to go wash as they came through the door. By this time Grams and I were really into the laughter. Gramps came back to the table with a big grin on his face trying not to laugh while asking, "What's so funny?"

"You Guys," Grams said while laughing, "When it comes to food I don't really need a bell,"

Gramps joined the laughter too.

Strong Bow and Elmosa (Mosa) came into the room just as Gramps started laughing and they were trying their best not to laugh. The harder they tried to hold it back the louder the snorts and snickers came till they both almost busted with laughter.

It took a few keptrons (minutes) for the laughter to slow down enough that we could all sit down to lunch.

Grams said, "A good laugh helps with digestion and is good for the soul."

"I totally agree," chimed in Gramps, "And lunch looks great. Say grace, Strong Bow so we can dig in."

Soon lunch was finished and the kitchen was clean once again.

"Time for me to be getting over to the Science Center and see how things are going," I said loud enough for everyone to hear. It was our custom for everyone to rest awhile after eating before going back to work.

"Ok, but remember what I told you and we agreed to," Strong Bow said giving me a hug and a few kisses.

"Yes, I remember and I did promise," I said starting down the steps, "Love all of you, see you this ponacron (evening)." I said waving to everyone on the porch.

While walking to the Science Center I wondered what kind of safety measures could be put in place to keep me and other travelers safe on these missions.

As I opened the oversized door to the front of the Science Center, I could see people hurrying around taking care of things like a bunch of ants on hot sand. I walked forward and through the doors opening into the Creation Dome.

"Oh good, you're here. I have the recordings up and ready to run. I need you to watch them and see if all of the information was retrieved correctly," Enah 2 (E 2) announced upon seeing me.

He had a chair and headgear set up so I could be near the holographic console. Part of me wanted to make sure that all of the data was recorded, but another part of me was dreading the idea of seeing myself floating in space again. Then the thought came that maybe it stopped recording before I drifted into space. I sat down and started the program.

"Oh good, it did record Nika (Nicky)'s song. Enah 2 (E 2)! Is there a way to record this song so I can hear it again later?" I asked, getting his attention.

"Yes, anything you want to record put this in the console and it will record automatically," he said handing me a small gold disk.

"Thank you," I said taking it from his

hand. The disk was only about the size of a small coin. I backed up the records so I could record the whole trip. I figured there would be a time when I would like to see it again or maybe Grams may want to.

I finally made it through the part where I was stuck in space and was surprised to see it did record the being I saw while there. I had started to wonder if he was part of a dream. The program had even recorded the thud of the chair being jolted during the quake. I am guessing that is when the power went off.

"This recorder is great. It even recorded the chair being jolted as the helmet fell off," I almost shouted to Enah 2 (E 2).

"That is great, did you make a record of it to file here?" he asked.

"Doing it now," I said as I slid in another gold disk. I put my copy in a protective sleeve and slid it into my pocket for safe keeping. "Anything else I can help with? I have a while before I will be needed at home," I volunteered.

"Yes, you can start in that area and make sure that all of our programs are put back in the proper order," he said pointing to the far side of the dome. The dome is on, so you don't have to worry about running out of time," he laughed.

"Good to know. That area looks to be quite a mess. Oh, did Strong Bow tell you I had to promise I wouldn't go on any more missions until safety programs and power units were put into place?" I asked.

"Yes and he has already took the idea to the Science Council and they all agreed that it was an excellent idea. It will protect all of our time data travelers," he explained with a smile, "I agreed with the idea. So we will be on hold for about a pestron (week). Everything should be repaired by that time and all back in place with anchors to keep them stable."

"Now that sounds like a very good idea," I laughed as I sat the cabinet back upright and stacked all of the disks so I could sort them easier. 'Hum, should I sort by continent and category first then by letters or the other way around? Really, either way will work. Just need to get started.'

I finally got all of the programs put in the proper order. I used Nika (Nicky)'s song to help me by singing it in my head while working. It seemed to give me the energy I needed to complete the task. I wonder if that is why she sang it so much. It was as if I could recall things of that time that I didn't live during this last visit.

"All of the programs are sorted and filed in the proper order. Anything else you need me to help with?" I asked.

"I heard Kerzna (Kern) was planning on starting a family and living with you and your family," Enah 2 (E 2) said walking across the room to me.

"Yes, he is looking for a mate. Last I heard his planet is helping him find the one that is suited to him. If I understand it right they do a match according to a lot of test that are run on each of them at about three sectos (years) of age. Then they add changes that they have experienced in life to this point. That helps them find just the right mate. He likes and understands the rules his people live by. Elmosa (Mosa) is helping him build the house," I explained.

"Yes I know their culture and I have heard from the council and if they got the message right, she is on our planet now, but is helping a family with their children for the next secto (year). So he can sort of take his time building the house. If I know the rules, she gets the last say in what it looks like and the arrangement inside," he said with a smile.

"I'm glad to hear that she is on our planet. Does he know this yet?" I ask.

"I'm not sure. I would think that the council got word to him this sestron (today)," he said, "Here is another crate of programs to add to the others you just finished, and there is another one over there."

"Okay," I laughed, "I'll get right on it."

I got them all sorted and put in their proper places. I know that time flows differently in the Domes that it does in real time outside, but it must be getting close to dinner time. I was starting to feel hungry.

"I think that is it for me today. I can come in the morning and help finish up. Do you think we will be ready to put the safety programs and the power units into place by tostron (tomorrow)?" I ask, looking over my shoulder on my way to the door.

"Yes, I think we may be to that point by noon tostron (tomorrow)," Enah 2 (E 2) said with a slight wave.

On the way to Gram's house I caught myself singing Nika (Nicky)'s song, I patted my pocket assuring myself I still had the disk.

Grams had dinner on the table when I got there and everyone was sitting at the table. I washed and sat down. Everyone looked at me as if waiting for me to say something.

"What? Did something happen here this sestron (day)?" I asked looking at each one of them in turn.

"No, just wondering what news you have for us," Grams said with a grin.

"I'm not sure what you mean. Most of the repairs are done in the time lab and I spent most of my day sorting and filing programs. I also recorded the trip I took sacytron (yesterday). Also was told that Kernza's mate is on this planet, but has a job for another year. Well that's all I know," I said with a grin. "So what happened here this sestron (day)?" I asked.

"Not much, we just wanted to hear how things went at the Science Center. Gramps heard that the information that you got on your trip help the council out a lot. It gave them the direction they needed for what safety programs and power packs to put into place. Because of what you went through on your trip - all of our time traveler will be safer now," Grams explained. "Let's eat while it is warm," she added with a laugh.

Story time went around the table as usual and each person told what had happened or what they had learn that sestron (day). Then it was time to clean up, visit a little more and then off to sleep land for everyone. Morning found Elmosa (Mosa) outside on the ground, where he had fallen asleep next to Kerzna (Kern) under the stars that night.

After a great breakfast each of us went out to do the best we could on the job at hand. Elmosa (Mosa) was helping Kerzna (Kern) make the house even though they didn't really have to hurry. Strong Bow and Gramps had things on the farm and in town they had to take care of. Grams was to teach a small art class on the front porch and I was off to help in the Science Center. This sestron (day) we will be adding the safety programs and power supplies to our systems, and learning how they work.

Chapter Three
Prison Planet

"Hello Elaytay (Tay). You are just in time. Mayler (Lar) just finished adding the safety programs in the data bases and they have up graded the power units, so there is a constant power feed no matter what happens," Enah 2 (E 2) explained.

"Thank you Mayler (Lar)." I said with a bow. "I am glad to hear these are all in place, and you are sure that if the power grid goes down all over the planet that these data bases and the times travel research units will still have power?" I said wanting to clarify.

"Yes, they have a backup of power for eight decons (hours), which should give you enough time to finish whatever you are doing.. There is also a warning signal that will chirp in your left ear when the backup power is being used," he informed me.

"That is good to hear. I like the idea of a warning system having a sound that I can hear," I said giving him a nod.

"Are you ready for your next assignment?" Enah 2 (E 2) ask.

"Sounds good, where am I off to this time?" I asked.

"The council needs more info on the displacement of planetary trouble makers after the forming of the United Planet Alliance. So you will be on the planet picked as a prison planet for the lack of a better name. Oh, I have to let you know, if you are an observer on this trip it is harder for us to see and hear what is happening. So if you can describe and explain things it will make it easier for us to piece together what we are seeing and hearing," Enah 2 (E 2) informed me.

"Sounds interesting, but dangerous," I said.

"Well remember that your physical body is here safe and sound. That thought should help," he said with a slight smile.

"Well ok, if they must have the info," I said while sitting down in the chair and putting the helmet on.

"Ok take a few long slow deep breaths," he instructed me.

"Wow! I hope you are seeing ALL of this," I relayed to Enah 2 (E 2) as I became aware of what was happening and where I was.

"I'm on a planet that seemed to be very active. There are bubbling mud pots almost at every turn. I seem to be without a body this time. I guess I can just stand where ever I want to without being notice, because a young man and a very old one just walked past me while passing through my arm. I am standing on a very narrow path between mud pots and hot springs. There are a few caves in the side of a cliff that this path seems to lead to. I'm going to investigate.

The first cave seems to be the dwelling place of the young man and the very old man." I reported.

"Did you say that this was the planet where the trouble makers were sent? Do we know what planets sent their peoples to this planet? And how long ago did they start using this planet?" I asked Enah 2 (E 2).

"All of them did at the time, but I think that each of them had their own areas that they used. And supplies were dropped from the air or beamed down for the first secto (year). After that they were pretty much on their own. I think that the first peoples there were over two sectos (years) ago" Came the answer loud and clear.

"Well they seem to be doing pretty well. They have managed to get a small garden going. I am thinking that the heat from the springs should let it grown almost all year long. I am hearing some very strange sounds, like roars and thumping. What kind of things are on this planet, animal wise I mean?" I asked Enah 2 (E 2).

"We don't know. No one ever landed

there to find out how the people they left there did. They were just beamed down and left without any contact after that except for the supply drops. There was no way to contact them because leaving them with any communication electron equipment was against the rules set up by the United Planetary Alliance. That is why you are there is to find out as much as you can," he said.

"Ok, I will find out as much as I can," I said walking into the cave where the young and older man was.

"It seems that these two have found a fuel source to use other than wood. It seems to be droppings from a very large animal. They have food and they are wearing clothes made of animal skins. Wait a female just came in carrying a very large, (I paused to take a closer look) well it looks like a scale from a telnazar (lizard). It is so large that it is almost half as big as her. I am thinking this is now a family unit. How long ago were the first people left here?" I reported and asked.

"I am not really sure of the exact dates, but I know that it is close to several generations. They didn't really notice any people of higher intelligence on the planet and that is one of the reasons they picked this one," he replied.

"Ok, well that would make sense then that this would be a family. She does look a little different than the old man does. It seems she may be from a different planet. She is a little darker and her reactions when he asked for things are as if she is still trying to figure out what he wants. I think I am going to visit the next cave," I said.

"It seems that the peoples from several planets are living in this area. The people in this next cave have a lot more body hair and don't wear as much clothing as the last family did. They are smaller than the people in the first cave. I don't know if they are just small or children, but they can jump pretty high and climb real good. They seemed to be able to scramble fast, because when this other male walked into the cave they took what they were eating and climbed to the upper parts of the cave. He is now demanding them to give him the food they have. So I am thinking that this has happened before. Not sure what planet he comes from. He has a sort of green tinted skin, straight black hair with red stripes and an almost pointed head. He has a red braided beard and seems very impatient. He is acting like a bully. The larger of the two is giving him what he wants and he is leaving now. The bully couldn't reach the young ones.

As I look around and can see there are drawings on the walls. The younger male is very good at drawing and it seems to be a way of recording the important things that happen to them.

The mom and dad came in now and are

sharing a little food that had been hidden; this is another good reason for thinking that this happened pretty often. The ones I think are the mom and dad aren't much larger than the small ones

I am going to look in the next cave," I reported.

"As I walk out of this last cave, I am hearing another deep roar. I wish I knew what is making that sound. I can get a better look at the cliff wall now and there are a lot of caves in this area. The paths leading to them are winding through hot mud pots and hot springs. Then when you get to the cliff face the paths leading to each of the caves are just wide enough for two people to pass each other.

I'm starting to climb one of the paths and I just had a large shadow move over me. I am glad I can't be seen at times like this.

Wait! I didn't think I could be seen. I'm just an observer this time. AAAh! oh wow, that was a close one. I am stuck in a crack between caves. I was almost picked up by a toraducktis (pterodactyl). I will have to wait till he goes away to make my way to the next cave," I said.

"You are unseen and only an observer. But on this planet there must be some animals that can see past what people can see," Enah2 (E 2) said.

"You mean like Z 's Tapnah that animal could track anything and see a lot of things we couldn't see?" I said.

"Yes just like that," Enah 2 (E 2) replied.

"Great that would have been nice to know before almost getting pluck like a fruit," I said with what I could muster as a laugh. "I haven't studied the hunting habits of the toraducktis (pterodactyl). Does anyone there know how long it will take for him to give up and hunt somewhere else?" I asked.

"Not really. Our records don't include that information. We didn't think that kind of life was on that planet," Enah 2 (E 2) replied.

"What looked like a big green ball just rolled past me. Maybe it will take it and fly away so I can get out of this crack and get on with my investigations," I said while keeping an eye on the flying monster.

"Keep us posted," came Enah 2 (E 2)'s response.

"Wow it picked up the green ball and flew away. I'm on my way to the next cave. The people that live in this cave have a light gray tone to their skin. They are very tall and well built. I am seeing pictures on their walls of darnosus (dinosaurs) of all kinds. One is of a shorter person standing in from of a tagosup (triceratops) and the next is of what looks like the man commanding it. The last picture is of a man riding asagatonpots (stegosaurus), he is sitting among the spinal armor. Wow, this is fascinating. This may be the way they have learned to live here. So the deep roars I was hearing could have been darnosus (dinosaurs).

I am not hearing these people talk aloud or
moving their mouths. They are thinkers. I am
wondering if they may be the ones who help to
train the animals.

One of them is looking straight at me as
if he can see me. I think he can see me." I
reported.

'*Can you see me,*' I asked the one looking
at me.

'*Yes, ever so lightly almost as an outline,
but I can make you out. Why are you here?*' he
asked.

'*I was sent to learn a little more about what
happened during this time on this planet. Can you
answer questions for me? I am not here to make any
changes, just to learn and observe,*' I explained.

'*I can answer questions for you. My brother
is a history keeper and my sister helps to train the
animals. We have heard you talking to your people
since you got here, but didn't see you until now. The
green ball came from us,*' he informed me.

'*Wow, well thank you very much. So tell me
how humanoids have managed to live this long on
this planet?*' I asked.

'*It hasn't been easy. We still have a few
bullies among us. But they are bullies because it is
in their nature to be that way. It isn't because they
need the food or want for anything that anyone else
has. We know all that goes on in our community
and we knew when you first got here,*' he informed
me. '*By the way I am called Lantos (Tos), this is my
brother Brothos (Bro) and our sister Handos (Hans)
and you are called?*'

'Oh, I am known as Elaytay (Tay). I am a time traveler from Cyterrious, many years into your future. I am here to gather information on the history here,' I replied.

'Well, I can give you the quick highlighted version of all of this since our group was sent here,' he replied.

'Okay, do you have any ideas about the others on this planet?' I asked.

'We know a little about the others, but not their whole history. A lot of them weren't real good at keeping their history. Said they wanted to forget it and start anew life here with each generation,' he explained as he displayed a hand towards his brother Brothos (Bro).

'Yes well, our family was placed here about eight generation ago now for economic problems, to put it as general as I can. Our planet like most dropped supplied each time period for about a year. Then we were on our own and it was up to us to make friends, groups or communities or get eaten or die of starvation. We managed to find this plateau and it already had a few caves in its side with one path leading to the top. We all worked together and made more paths to get to the other hand made caves. The hot mud pot and hot water geysers with the narrow paths leading between them were an extra bonus from nature. We live by only a few rules. The main one is to do no harm to others and so far our community has done well by that one. There's one group that gets a little rowdy once in a while like being a bully, but the food and items are replaced or given back.

We have managed to train some of the animals so we have food as needed, and some help to haul supplies that helps make life a little better. The planets that dropped off their trouble makers (as they called us) didn't perform a very good recon on this planet before doing the drops. This planet already had humanoids on it. They may have looked different from us and may not have passed the intelligence test we gave our young, but they were smart enough to have survived on this planet for many generations before we got here. In fact the wife of the first family you visited is a half breed from here and another planet second generation. The second cave you visited is a family that was already living here when our planets dumped everyone. We learned a lot of survival ideas from their people,' he said.

I looked around while he was talking to me and noticed that their sister was no longer in the cave with us.

'Oh, I see you noticed our sister left. She is off to help our hunters gather meat that is needed for the colder months that will be coming in about another nine full moons. It takes time to prepare it,' Lantos (Tos) informed me.

About the time I was going to ask how they do all of that, loud and scary noises started coming from above on the Plateau. It sounded like a huge fight. Not long after I first heard the fight something big fell over the side of the Plateau.

"What was that," I asked running to the mouth of the cave to get a better look.

'It was a rextamo (tyrannosaurus). It fell

a great distance from the Plateau and looked like it has broken its neck.' He explained.

"All of the people are rushing from their caves to help cut up the rextamo before other animals smell the kill. Are you able to hear the communications between me and Lantos (Tos) and his family," I asked Enah 2 (E 2).

"Yes we can follow your thoughts pretty much and I know that you can fill in the few spots that need clarification," he replied.

I watched as they cut away the hide and carved the meat from the bones. *'How, uh. What is done with all of this to keep it from going bad?'* I asked looking over my shoulder at Lantos (Tos).

'We dry most all of it and then keep it in one of the deeper caves where we store a lot of our foods. We have found that you can dry fruits and vegetables the same way and later they make really good soups. We have found patches of grain bearing plants and we have found ways of making drinks from fruits and they are stored in hollowed stones coated inside with nut oils to keep them from seeping out of the stone jars,' he explained.

'We have learned a lot since our fore fathers were first dropped here,' Brothos (Bro) boasted with a large smile. *'We have found that if we cook some of the meat right off that it will keep for a good long time. The skins can be used for many different things; the bones are used for tools, furniture, and buildings and trading. Just to mention a few things,'* he added.

"I'm making my way closer to the cave

entrance so I can see clearly over the edge at what was happening below. All of the families seem to be working together to save as much meat as they can.

They have made a way to put a large portion of one leg into one of the hot springs using what looks like ropes. I had noticed on my way past the springs that they seem to be freshwater hot springs they don't stink like the ones I remember learning about." I reported to Enah 2 (E 2).

Just then I heard a loud screech just over head and all of a sudden there was screams and people running in all directions along the paths carrying all that they could through the paths.

"All of the people are running for their cave carrying as much meat as they could carry while trying not to be attack. The screeching is getting louder and now the shadows of two toraducktis (Pterodactyl) were flying in circles over the hot springs and mud pots." I explained to Enah 2 (E 2).

'They will circle three times before landing. That is the reason everyone grabbed what they could carry and started running,' Lantos (Tos) said

One of the geysers went off and almost hit the one that was making its last circle, but was able to dodge the hot spray. They let the people run with what they had because there was still a lot of meat left for them.

'What is Handos (Hans) doing down there with the toraducktis (Pterodactyl)?' I asked, looking over at Lantos (Tos).

'She has this idea that she can train them to let her ride them. And she finally had enough leather and rope saved to make a mouth muzzle and safety seat. We tried to talk her out of it yesterday but she was determined to make it work,' he explained.

"I am standing on the edge of the path not really believing what I am watching. I hope you are seeing this." I told Enah 2 (E 2).

'Is there anything you can do to help her?' I asked looking at both of her brothers.

'Not from here,' they said as they crept down the paths toward the base.

I followed them almost holding my breath with each step. I wanted my steps to be silent.

'If we can get a little closer then maybe we can help make them relaxed and they will trust us with a full belly. At least that is the hope,' Brothos (Bro) said looking back at me.

The one nearest to us was the one that Handos (Hans) had chosen to try and ride. Its eyes were almost closed. She slipped on the soft head gear and lead ropes and it seemed to almost be falling asleep while she hurried to slip on a soft leather harness around the wings making an X across its back. This X had holes in it to put her feet through and a body belt that went around her. As she climbed onto its back, it opened its eyes and screeched.

This screech alerted the one next to it and it flew straight up. Handos (Hans)'s brother ran very fast towards the first cave.

I started to run also. My heart beating so

fast I felt it was going to out run me. I glanced up when I say this huge shadow cover me.

"Aahhugh!" I screamed.

Its feet clamped around me and it flew up and over the Plateau. I held on for dear life. I'm so scared I reached out and grabbed one toe just as it opened its claw..

"I'm being carried in the air by a toraducktis (pterodactyl)," I informed Enah 2 (E 2).

"Are you ok? Are you hurt?" he asked.

"Not that I am aware of, but I am too scared to look right now. I'm not sure what he has in mind. Two of them just got through with a large meal, so I am hoping for the best," I said. "I am seeing other villages below," I informed him.

"Check your right arm for bleeding," he said.

"Yes there is blood. How did you know?" I asked.

"Because it is showing up on your arm here. It's not bad and we can take care of it, so not to worry," he informed me.

"Handos (Hans) is riding the other toraducktis (pterodactyl) and she is coming up under me it looks like," I informed Enah 2 (E 2).

"Who is doing what?" he asked.

"I will tell you all after I get out of this mess," I said as Handos (Hans) got under me.

"Drop!" she screamed aloud.

We were flying real high at this point and I was shaking so bad it was hard to control myself. I didn't dear look past her at the ground. I had made sure up till now that I was looking out in front of me so I could keep my head.

"What!" I said cupping one ear with my free hand.

His wings were making a roaring sound as he flew.

"Get loose and drop! Drop! Now! I will catch you!" she screamed even louder. "It is either that or be eaten later," she yelled, waving for me to drop.

I struggled to get my clothes loose from the one claw. I managed to pull up the one toe and I bit it as hard as I could. The claws opened and I was now tumbling through the air.

I'm falling with my back towards the ground. I can't see Handos (Hans). I don't know if she is there for me or not. Waving my arms and twisting my body I managed to turn over.

The Earth is coming toward me fast and I'm not seeing Handos (Hans). I can hear myself screaming.

"I'm falling and…" fighting to catch my breath. "Tell everyone there I love them but I may not make it back this time," I screamed at Enah 2 (E 2).

Just then Handos (Hans) flew in under me and I managed to catch hold of her hand.

"Hold on and we will land. Try to hold on," she shouted while placing my hands on the ropes that were tied to her seat.

"Oh don't worry I am holding on with everything I have," I shouted back.

Not long after that we landed just outside the hot springs and mud pot maze.

I dropped off onto the ground. While her brothers came running to meet her. As she talked to them she took all of the riding gear she had made off of the toraducktis (pterodactyl

While they were talking I decided to let Enah 2 (E 2) in on all that I had managed to find out so far.

Handos (Hans) offered the toraducktis (pterodactyl) more food and talked to it while stroking its neck. So far it seemed ok with what was happening.

The toraducktis (pterodactyl) flew away as Handos (Hans) and her brothers walked away.

I am on my way to investigate the other caves. There are running noises behind me. When I turn, Lantos (Tos) is catching up with me.

'So where are you going now? I bet what you just went through was very scary,' he suggested.

'Yes it was. I thought my heart was going to jump out of my chest a few times. But I need to get on with my investigations and report back to my people what I have found out. So I need to check out the other caves,' I said.

'I can help you there. I visit with everyone here and know all of them. The cave next in line is Krownosas (Kro). He is head of our medical team. His sons help in taking care of all of us. We have all learned to watch out for each other. There are other groups and colonies within three days walk of here but most are of a warrior tribe.

"Greeting Krownosas (Kro), how are things going this day? Did everyone fair okay after all the excitement?" asked Lantos (Tos).

"Oh yes, everyone did good. Just a few minor scratches, but nothing close to last time," Krownosas (Kro) answered with a smile.

"I see your son is working on bones. What is he doing?" Lantos (Tos) asked.

"He is studying how they are made and the different parts. It is part of his education. He needs to learn everything I know so he will have a base to add to as new information comes available," Krownosas (Kro) explained.

I'm standing near Lantos (Tos) so I can hear and see all that is happening.

'So you see how things work here,' Lantos (Tos) said to me looking in my direction.

'Yes I am learning,' I said with a smile.

Krownosas (Kro) was a rather short lean man with a slight yellow tint to his skin, straight black hair and dark eyes. His son looked to be about fourteen years of age. But I didn't see a female in this family.

The cave didn't have many comforts. There was a few placed near the floor to sleep in the warmer weather and a few more above carver out of the wall. There was a fire pit near the door so that the smoke could flow to the outside. The walls were decorated with flowers and trees, the kind of things you would have maybe found on their home planet.

'Is there a female for this family?' I asked looking at Lantos (Tos).

'There was but she was killed by one of the warrior clansmen after she helped Krownosas (Kro) fix his broken leg. From that time he only helps our immediate group,' Lantos (Tos) said.

"Blessings," Lantos (Tos) said with a slight wave as he turned and walked out of the cave.

'The next cave is that of Kransdel (Cran), our scientist and inventor,' Lantos (Tos) explained as we walked up the path to the next cave.

It was slightly larger than the last one. It seemed that the larger cave were closer to the Plateau.

As we got closer we were overtaken by a horrible smell and horrendous noise.

"Hello!" Lantos (Tos) yelled over the noise. "What are you working on this day?" Lantos (Tos) asking while looking around.

"I'm melting down some soft metal chips I found," Kransdel (Cran) yelled back.

"What is all of that noise?" Lantos (Tos) yelled through cupped hands.

"Oh," Kransdel (Cran) laughed, "That's my son and his rock crusher," he added.

"What are you going to make with the metal?" questioned Lantos (Tos) moving closer so he would hear better.

"Communications. At least that is what I have planned," Kransdel (Cran) said with a large grin while holding up a good sized box. "I figure it's about time to try and get in touch with at least one of the planet that helped start this idea," he added.

"Do you really think you have a chance?" Lantos (Tos) questioned.

"I managed to hang on to some old computer components that have been passed on to me from my great grandparents and they got them from their grandparents. They came from the ships the original groups landed here in. They were only fueled with enough to land them safely but not enough to take off again. The fuels that were in the drop shipments after they landed were not the right fuels for the ships," Kransdel (Cran) explained.

"That make sense, understanding the way things were then," Lantos (Tos) said with a nod. "I will leave you to your work then. See you later," he added with a wave.

'Ok we are headed for the last and highest cave. It belongs to Ganfarnel (Gan), he is our grower of foods (farmer),' Lantos (Tos) explained.

As we grew closer to Ganfarnel (Gan)'s cave I could see that he had made a wider landing in front of his cave.

"I am going to see Ganfarnel (Gan). He

has managed. to start his cave farther back in the face of the Plateau so he has room to start plants. I noticed the rows of what looked like small ditched along the paths earlier, but didn't really think much about them. Now they made sense to me. They are used to plant the food crops in. He has managed like Krownosas (Kro) did to save and learn as much as he could from his parents and grandparents as he could about their trade. After all they had managed to survive in a strange place for many generations, so they must be right about something. He has been taught how to gather seeds from each crop that is planted for the following year." I explained to Enah 2 (E 2).

'You see this aplose (apple) tree growing here?' asked Lantos (Tos).

'Yes,' I answered wondering where he was going with the question.

'I have often wondered a few things about how Ganfarnel (Gan) manages these things and still keeps us safe,' he continued.

"Ganfarnel (Gan)," he yelled to call him to the front of the cave. "I see this aplose (apple) tree growing just outside your cave. How do you keep the peoples from other places from climbing down the tree and invading what we have built?" he asked.

"Very easily," came Ganfarnel (Gan)'s answer. "I cut back certain branches. If you look closely at the tree you will see that it is shorter than the top of the Plateau by about twelve feet and the branches are hanging out away from the Plateau. So if anyone was to try and jump to the tree, those limbs wouldn't hold them and they would fall and get hurt really bad. Maybe even die." he continued.

"Oh," Lantos (Tos) said while looking closely at the tree. "Good I've been wondering about that for some time now. Thank you for explaining that. What new things have you planted for us?"

"Well on my scouting trip I did last week I found what I believe to be a fruit that is eatable by humans. Mancol (Man) went with me and he found it. He is still alive after eating it. So I am thinking it should be ok for the rest of us to eat," Ganfarnel (Gan) related to me with a chuckle.

"Mancol (Man)?" Lantos (Tos) questioned.

"Oh," Ganfarnel (Gan) laughed. "Mancol (Man) is what I call the male of the original family. After all we haven't found a foundation for their language if you want to call it that. At least I haven't, so I call him Mancol (Man). He seems to like it," he added.

"I agree they are of very few words but they communicate in different ways. Parts of it is even mind to mind and the sounds are to emphasize the thought or urgency," Lantos (Tos) explained.

"Thank you, I always wondered about that. That alone explains a lot," Ganfarnel (Gan) said.

"Well, getting back to what we found. Here take a look. I brought back a whole bag full," he said handing Lantos (Tos) what I know as a reapa (pear).

"Go ahead, take a bite, they are sweet but the texture is different from the aplose (apple)," he said warningly.

Lantos (Tos) took a bite. "It is sweet and taste pretty good but the texture is very strange and will take a bit of getting used to," he said looking toward me and smiled before looking back at the fruit.

"I am hoping that I can get one of these trees to grow here for all of us," Ganfarnel (Gan) said.

"Thank you for showing me this and explaining about the tree," Lantos (Tos) said as we turned to leave. "See you later," he said with a wave.

'Where are you going now?' I asked.

'I was thinking that you might want to learn a little more about Mancol (Man) and his family,' Lantos (Tos) said.

'Sure, but how,' I questioned.

'I will figure that out as we go,' he said walking down the path a little faster.

The path was a little steeper at this point and with his long legs he had gotten far enough away that I had to run to catch up.

"Mancol (Man)," Lantos (Tos) yelled as he got closer to their cave.

Mancol (Man) came running out to see who it was.

'*Is that your real name? I mean is that what you are called?*' Lantos (Tos) said to him using telepathy.

Mancol (Man) shrugged his shoulders. '*Better than ugg,*' he said.

'*Where did you live before this cave?*' Lantos (Tos) asked.

I then realized that he knew most of the answers to the questions he was asking and was asking them so I could hear the answers. So I just smiled when he looked over at me.

Mancol (Man) looked in my direction and made a motion towards me. '*Let speak*' he said.

'*Can you see her?*' Lantos (Tos) asked.

'*No, but know spirit. Can feel,*' he said pointing again in my direction.

'*Can you hear me when I speak?*' I asked.

'*Yes,*' came his answer quickly.

'*Wow, that is great,*' I said '*I have so many questions.*'

'*How long have you lived in this cave?*' I asked.

'*Many fathers ago,*' he said motioning us to follow him into the cave.

On one wall was just hand prints, most of them were from the right hand. I counted them as he motioned to them making grunting sounds, there were twelve.

'*Many fathers,*' he finally said.

'*How long do your fathers live?*' I asked

trying to get some idea how long they had
lived in that cave. Then I notices lines carved in
the rock under each hand.

He patted the lines and said *'Cold,'*
'Lantos (Tos) does he mean winters?' I
asked.

Mancol (Man) tilted his head and
looked at Lantos (Tos).

*'Macol (winter), cool time, ice, not hunting.
Macol (winter),'* Lantos (Tos) said.

Mancol (Man) nodded yes, "Ma cool?"
he said aloud.

I looked under each hand and their lives
averaged about thirty-four years. That is not to
say some of them lived for a very long time and
some dies earlier. That means that his family
had lived in this cave for around four hundred
years. I had to agree, it was one of the safer
places to be. Unless you were to live
underground like Nenapol who's relay station I
had found on my second mission to Earth and I
had been told his group wasn't the only ones
who lived underground.

Just then his children came running
through the cave and laughing. I had to laugh,
they seemed to be having so much fun. One
had caught a bird and he let it go after he got
well into the cave.

Mancol (Man) nodded and laughed too.

*'So when did Lantos (Tos) and his group
join you here?'* I asked.

He pointed at the third father in, and

then pointed to the last hand print and patted himself on the chest. So I would think that it was a little over two hundred and fifty years ago.

'*Does about two hundred and fifty years sound about right to you?*' I asked looking at Lantos (Tos).

'*Yes I would think that would be about right,*' he answered. '*But you know Elijos (Elijah) would know for sure, because his family was among the first ones to be left here. The law enforcers figured we needed a spiritual guide and his family was the one they picked for our group,*' he added.

I thanked Mancol (Man) for all of his help and we left to go visit with Elijos (Elijah).

Elijos (Elijah)'s cave was only about seventy-five feet from Mancol (Man)'s, so as we got closer Lantos (Tos) called out to him.

"Elijos (Elijah), are you home?" Lantos (Tos) yelled.

"Yes, I will be out in a few," he answered. "Yes, what can I help you with?"

"Well, I have a few questions I have always wondered about. Do you have time to set and talk?" Lantos (Tos) asked.

"Sure, I always have time to talk to one of our group," he said quickly while looking back into the cave.

To me that seemed a little strange. It was as if he was trying to hide something. So I walked into the cave to look around. I hadn't really noticed anything right away, but I wasn't really looking for anything special. But there was something he may want to hide from the rest.

The boy that was helping him was busy covering things with the furs that are laid out for seating and beds. I need to get closer to see what he is covering up. It looks like an old chest from a starship. Looks like I may have to stay here a little after Lantos (Tos) leaves.

"Can we go inside?" Lantos (Tos) asked.

Elijos (Elijah) looks into the cave again and the boy gives him a nod. "Sure, come on in and sit for a while," he offered.

They both came in and sat near the door where it was cooler today.

"I have been meaning to ask you how long you have been on this planet?" Lantos (Tos) asked.

"As you know I am part of a religious order and there were a group of us put into place before they started dropping off what the enforcers considered trouble makers," he said.

"Yes, go on," Lantos (Tos) agreed.

"Well I am part of the third wave to be left here. We have all had special training in the things that needed to be taught to all of the peoples. And I am here to teach everyone in our group. Our group is smaller now than it was at one point. There were a few families that didn't want to listen to anything I had to say and refused to follow the ways that had been laid out before people were brought here. They decided to move out on their own and a lot of them perished because of it. This is one of the few safe places on this planet right now. I think my kind have been here a little over two hundred and fifty years," he explained.

"Did your leaders ever say when or if they were coming back for you or the others?" Lantos (Tos) asked point blank.

"No, why do you ask about that?" Elijos (Elijah) asked looking straight at Lantos (Tos).

"I was just wondering if you had electronic or mechanical components that you had shared with anyone?" Lantos (Tos) said trying to choose his words carefully.

"No, I haven't given anything to anyone. I do experiment with what my people called alchemy. I dabble in religious science, miracles now and again. Why do you ask?" he asked again.

"Just wondering, no real reason. I know that you know things before they happen and was trying to figure out how you know just in time to help save us all from harm," answered Lantos (Tos) trying not to give too much information.

Meanwhile I was looking around and trying to get a peek at things under the furs without lifting or moving them too far and being noticed. The old starship chest I had caught a glimpse of earlier had something written on it but it was in a different language that I hadn't learned yet. I tried to take a closer look at it hoping that Ehan 2 could see it and translate it for me.

I stepped outside to ask Enah 2 (E 2), "Did you get a clear enough picture of the starship chest and the writing on it to tell me what it said," I asked.

"It was hard to make out but I think we seen enough of it to get a translation. I will have it for you in a few keptrons (minutes). Yes here it is, (Galatorc communications). That planet was metamorphosed to a different vibration and isn't seen in our realm anymore," he said. "But in the time you are visiting, that hasn't happened yet," he added.

"Good to know. Thank you," I said before walking back into the cave.

"Thank you for the history lesson," Lantos (Tos) said shaking hands and giving a small bow to Elijos (Elijah).

"You are welcome anytime Lantos (Tos)," Elijos (Elijah) said bowing.

'I'm going to stay for a little while to see what happens when he doesn't think anyone is around,' I said as Lantos (Tos) passed me near the cave entrance.

'Ok, let me know later' Lantos (Tos) said.

I nodded and entered the cave. I decided to stand where I would be out of the way and where I could see most of what went on.

Elijos (Elijah) got out the chest and opened it. It was a communications system. He sent the boy to the cave door to sit and watch for anyone coming their way. I don't think he could hear what was being said from where he was. It was hard for me to hear but I didn't want to get any closer. Seems there was a large glacier headed their way and the Plateau was in its path. But they still had a few months to move. He put on a head set so he could hear things he didn't want the boy to hear. I needed to get a little closer to hear.

"Who is here?" Elijos (Elijah) said loudly while taking off the headset.

"What? I'm not seeing anyone," the boy answered.

"Answer me!" he commanded yelling even louder.

I had moved farther away when he yelled the first time.

"I am here to observe the happening of your time," I said timidly.

"Then come near that I might see you," he commanded.

At that he put on a special pair of glasses and then looked around the room.

"Ah, there you are. Come closer so I can get a good look at you," he demanded.

I don't feel good about this, but I move a little closer. My brain and gut was definitely in conflict. But I was going to try and stay out of reach.

'Lantos (Tos)! He can see me. He has glasses that can see me. COME HELP!' I shouted inside my mind to Lantos (Tos) hoping he could hear

me.

The boy had snuck up behind me and I hadn't noticed. He grabbed me and held onto me and before I had time to yell they had tied me up with a special tether that interrupted my monocular field and made me more physical.

"What are you going to do with me?" I asked, noticing that the boy now had on the same kind of glasses.

"Good job Ishuwa (Ish)," he said. Then looked at me, "You will see what happens to those who invade my privacy," he said.

"LANTOS (TOS)! HELP!" I screamed as loud as I could.

I was starting to get scared. I didn't know what would happen to me on the other side where my body was if something happened to me here.

Lantos (Tos) came running through the cave door about that time and broke the hold that Ishuwa (Ish) had on me. Just in time because I wasn't sure what Elijos (Elijah) had in mind.

"She is a historian, that's all. She doesn't mean any harm to any of us and isn't going to stop you from doing whatever you had planned," he said looking at the chest.

"Why didn't you tell me we had a spy among us?" Elijos (Elijah) asked.

"She isn't a spy. She is an observer that is all. She isn't here to change anything. What are you afraid of?" Lantos (Tos) asked.

'There was mention of a glacier from whoever is on the other end of the communications,' I explained to Lantos (Tos).

"Elijos (Elijah), is there a glacier coming this way?" Lantos (Tos) asked.

"Yes, but I was told there isn't enough time to get out of its way," he explained.

"Who were you talking to?" Lantos (Tos) asked.

"My group has had observers watching from the beginning of all of this, and they let me know a few things once in a while. My time here is almost up and that is why I have been training Ishuwa (Ish). He is to take my place when I am gone," he said looking in my direction.

"So were you going to tell any of us about this in time to move?" asked Lantos (Tos).

"I didn't find out about it till now, but there is a way out for all of us. But you have to do exactly what I tell you, and nothing less," Elijos (Elijah) said.

"OK, so what do we need to do?" asked Lantos (Tos).

"Have you sister bring in her pet talslemo (like a badger with very long claws). We will need his help to dig. I have been shown where the tunnels are that were made in the past," he confessed.

"Tunnels?" Lantos (Tos) questioned.

"Yes, there is a long tunnel system deep

underground and one of the tunnels runs within digging distance of us if we start on it right away," he explained.

"And what about my friend? Will you leave her alone? She is just an observer. Her people just wanted to know more about us and our way of life," he explained waiting for an answer.

"Yes, fine as long as she doesn't get in our way," he said.

"I promise. I will stay out of your way," I said quickly while taking off the tether.

"Have your sister here when the sun first shows," Elijos (Elijah) demanded, "We will be in need of all the time we have to pull off this escape," he continued.

"I will let her know," Lantos (Tos) said as we walked out of the cave.

Lantos (Tos) told his sister what Elijos (Elijah) said about needing her help and the help of her pet talslemo (like a badger with very long claws). When he told her about the digging she let Lantos (Tos) know that she also had made a pair of gloves with talslemo claws attached to them and that she would be able to dig also.

'I really want to see these tunnels Elijos (Elijah) was talking about,' I said.

'Yes I would like to know more about those tunnels also. I want to know who made them. We were supposed to have been the first people on this planet according to what we were told. We know that to be wrong because we found Mancol (Man)

and his family and they have been here for a lot longer than we have,' Lantos (Tos) said while looking at me, Brothos (Bro) and Handos (Hans).

We all nodded, and decided to ask Elijos (Elijah) first thing in the morning.

Out of the quietness of the evening was what sounded like a large explosion and a lot of commotion. We all got up and ran for the cave entrance. There in the near darkness was a bright light of orange, yellows and reds. It looked like a large fire in the sky and below it was Elijos (Elijah) with his hands raised. All of a sudden a beam of white light surrounded him and he started to rise into the sky and then he was gone. Seconds after he vanished what I think was a ship streaked out of sight.

"Well with Elijos (Elijah) gone all we can do is hope he told Ishuwa (Ish) where we were to dig. And just maybe he knows a little about the tunnels," Lantos (Tos) said walking back into the cave.

"I hope your right," Brothos (Bro) said spreading out his fur on the floor near the fire.

"Let's get some sleep and maybe it will all be better in the morning," said Handos (Hans) while petting Tawly her pet talslemo (like a badger with very long claws).

This was going to be my first time for spending the night while on a time mission, so I wasn't really sure what to expect. But I laid down on one of the furs and watched the fire until I drifted off. The next thing I know I was back in the Science Center and Enah 2 (E 2) was taking the helmet off of me.

"Well done Elaytay (Tay). The information you gathered help tremendously.

"Thank you but I wasn't able to find out who built the tunnels. Elijos (Elijah) left on a ship in the middle of the darkness," I said.

"Yes we saw all of that. But not to worry because our historians know who and when the tunnels were built," Enah 2 (E 2) informed me.

"So tell me, how long did this time trip take in our time?" I asked wondering if we had time for another trip today.

"Not long at all compared to some of the other trips that have been done here. I would say there is time for one more trip if you are up for it," Enah 2 (E 2) said with a grin.

Chapter Four
Saturn's Pet Problem

"Do you feel like taking another trip?" Enah 2 (E 2) asked looking over a panel at me.

"Good, let's do it," I said getting up to stretch and get a drink. "In about ten keptrons (minutes),"

"I have on my helmet and everything checks out here," I said giving Enah 2 (E 2) a thumbs up after sitting back down.

"Okay, lay back and relax and let it happen," he instructed.

"I'm finding myself on a space ship. I'm alone. This ship has only the one seat and I'm sitting in it as pilot. I am seeing a cargo area as I look around. I'm looking at my orders and the maps to see what I'm to do after I get to my destination. Seems I'm on my way to Saturn and the ship is on auto so I can look around," I relayed to Enah 2 (E 2).

'Seems I work for a company called Co-Pukapa and according to what I am reading they are known for repairing machines and mechanical AI devices of all kinds.

If I remember my histories, Saturn has been ruled by a King since their first planetary war. They were at war with one of their moons and after the dust settled, as the saying goes, a lot of their animals had gone extinct.

The King made an order to design and build mechanical animals to replace the ones that were lost during the war, especially his own favorite animals.

It's been a long time (about sixty sectos (years) since these animals were built and all of the King's technicians, mechanics and programmers have either died or left Saturn.

My boss received the transmission request about him needing the repairs done. The king wants all of his animals serviced and in working order before I leave. I'm hoping I have everything I'm going to need for the jobs ahead.

After landing I have to meet the king right off and need to see his special/personal collection first. The notes say there are a few that look like his personal pets.

Then I am to go to their version of our PAFOW (zoo) to do all of the repairs on the rest of the animals. It seems to me, if I remember the history right; their last war was fought with EMPs (electromagnetic pulses) and that is what disabled all of the embionics (electronics and powered functions) and the damage was to both sides. I am thinking that is what ended the war.

"I just landed and a greeting party is on its way to meet me," I explained to Enah 2 (E 2).

"Remember we can see and hear everything you see and hear," Enah 2 (E 2) whispered in my head.

"Oh yes, I forgot, "I said with a chuckle.

"Greetings, my name is Pokuna (Po), I am brother of His Grace. Welcome to Saturn reigned by Lord and King Rumonavar. I am most glad you are here. His Grace has been waiting your arrival most eagerly," he said bowing low.

As he straightened again he motioned for the others with him to gather all of the supplies and tools I had brought with me. "I am most assured that you will not be needing much of what you have brought. Our work areas are well supplied," he said as he motioned for me to walk with him.

"What can you tell me about the animals I will be working on and others that need repairs," I asked as we grew near the palace.

"My Sire has several favorite animals. There is a musolot, a nisomite, a hosmonie, a solaka, and a bodrooka just to name a few. Those are the ones that stay in the palace with His Grace. Oh! I don't know if you've been told they are all programed with artificial intelligence and they all can talk and hold conversations with anyone who is willing to talk to them, including each other audible and telepathically. It is most interesting to just stay out of sight and listen to their conversations," he informed me with a slight laugh while handing 3-D holopics (pictures) of each, while we walked to the palace.

"I wasn't given much information about the animals or the kinds of repairs I would be performing. But this helped me understand a little better. Can you tell me which are which, so I will know them when I see them," I asked holding up their pictures.

"Oh, well yes. You see, that one? Notice the rounded head with large orange and yellow eyes that almost look like fire, the long pointed ears that stand upright, a medium size body with short tan fur, and a short tail with a blue tip? That is a musolot (cat). The next one stands about the middle of my shins, has dark fur with green spots, has a long face with short ears, long tail, small red eyes, and notice the three long claws on each foot. This is a nisomite (dog). The third picture you are holding is of an animal with white fur, rainbow colored wings, an oval shaped head with pink floppy ears, a long tail, round black eyes and stands tall enough to look the King in the eyes, that is a hosmonie (winged horse). The next to the last one, has long black fur with yellow spots, bright green eyes, and oval face, large mouth and long fingers and toes. It has a long fuzzy tail and oversized round ears. This is called a

solaka (monkey). And the last picture you're
holding has a head that is almost square, large
oversized pale blue eyes, medium sized ears
that stick straight out from the sides of its head.
It has long fingers on its hands and four long
claws on its back feet. Its fur is purple with
brown spots or maybe it is brown with purple
spots, and a medium length tail with yellow
and purple stripes. This is a bodrooka
(raccoon)," he said letting out a loud sneeze just
as he finished describing the animals. "His
Grace is just up these stairs," he continued and
motioned for the supplies and tools to be taken
to their proper rooms.

     "My Lord Rumonavar," he said bowing
very low.

     I bowed as well. I wasn't really sure
what to do. I'd never worked for or ever met a
King.

     "This is Nekuma (Nick) the repair
person sent by Co-Pukapa to repair your
animals, My Lord," Pokuna (Po) said with his
head still facing the floor and one hand
outstretched toward me.

     I was watching his every move. As a
visitor one doesn't want to offend the leaders or
rulers of a country much less a whole planet.

     King Rumonavar clapped his hands for
us to rise. I am glad he did because neither of
us were looking at him. "No need to be so
formal when it is just the three of us in the
room. My name is Rumo two very close friends

and family but only in private settings. We will be working very closely together on the repairs.

"Thank you Rumo," I said smiling, "Please tell me about your pets and the other animals that are in need of help."

Just then the hosmonie (winged horse) entered the room. Its head was only as tall as me. It was able to move its front feet but it was dragging one back foot. It whinnied a greeting then I heard its voice in my head. "I am Rumonavar's grand hosmonie (horse). I was made strong enough to carry his grace from place to place, but the last few years I haven't been able to get my left rear leg to move correctly," he said and whinnied again.

It seemed odd that I could hear the conversation in my head but I didn't see the hosmonie's (horse) mouth move. So I asked him telepathically "Are you talking to me telepathically or am I really hearing an audible voice? And can everyone in the room hear what you just said?"

"Oh, I can talk either way and to all or just one. I have been programed to hold conversations either way. I have found that most humanoids blast their thoughts to all when talking and seem to have a very hard time talking to only one person. So when I enter a room where there are more than one humanoid I close off my telepathic translator so as not to hear all of these voices," he informed me, "Although there are a few humanoids that

I have come across who can send pictures while
they are talking and they are a little fun to
listen to. It is almost like watching a vid with
sound." he added. "You seem to be one of the
ones that talk and send pictures at the same
time." He added.

"Thank you for letting me know this. It
may be very useful when I start my repairs," I
said. "So why is it that you're programing
didn't get erased or damaged during the EMP
wars?" I asked.

"I was built with extra protection when
I received my last programing and repairs. That
was when EMP waves were first discovered,"
he informed me, "If I may make a request, I
would like very much to assist you in your
repairs. I have helped in the past with other
service personal?" he explained, while looking
towards the King for approval.

"If you wouldn't mind an onlooker with
suggestions once in a while, he may be of some
use in a few cases?" Rumo offered politely.

"I wouldn't mind at all if he wants to
help. By the way what is your name or do the
animals here have names?" I asked feeling a
little shy.

Rumo started laughing. "Yes of course
all of my animals have names. I am sorry. I had
totally forgotten the introduction the two of
you. This is Hasenaty (Hans) my pet hosmonie
(horse) And Hasenaty (Hans) this is Nekuma
(Nick) the repair person Co-pukapa sent to do

all of the repairs on the animals," he said while
pointing at each of us in turn with a full hand
palm up.

"Glad to meet you Hasenaty (Hans)," I
said with a large smile.

"And I you, Nekuma (Nick)," Hasenaty
(Hans) said with a nod of his head.

"It is getting late in the evening and the
lite leaves our area quickly. Our last meal will
be served soon and we will all retire and get an
early start when the light comes through this
window," Rumo announced pointing at a
special small round window at shoulder height
on one wall, "All of your tools and supplies are
in the main operations' unit at the far wing of
my palace," he added.

Soon we sat down at a very long table in
a gaily decorated room, full of vibrant colors
and strange animal murals on the walls. The
doorways were adorned with painted flowers
of all kinds, some having faces as if to say they
had personalities.

Sleep came easy, but I was rudely
awakened but what looked like a musolot (cat).
Its blue tipped tail was flipping me in the face
as it sat on the edge of the bed looking out the
window. "I guess it is time to get up," I said
raising my head off the pillow.

The musolot (cat) looked at me, made a
low rumbling sound turned, jumped off the
bed, and ran through the open door of the
room I was given to sleep in.

Hasenaty (Hans) (the horse) was passing by the bedroom door just as I got to it.

"The morning meal is being served in the dining room if you are hungry," he said, "I'll meet you in the operations' unit."

"Yes, thank you. I will be there shortly and we will have a look at you first," I offered with a slight wave as he turned to continue towards the far wing of the palace.

Before long I made my way to the operation's unit.

"Hasenaty (Hans), show me around and let's get started," I said smiling.

"Good I agree, the sooner the better." He replied.

"There's a lot to take in. Rumo is right the operation's unit is well supplied. I feel lucky Hasenaty (Hans) knows all of the equipment and is informing me as to what each instrument and machine is used for. I'm making notes on each one. You can read them when I look at them. Saturn's scientists were more advanced that I had been told. There are mechanical units that I have never dreamed of. I've studied and am sort of a pro when it came to repairs the old way. I had been trained to use my ears, eyes, instincts and intuition as to when things were out of sync. In this operation unit there are machines and instruments that are tuned to each and every part of an AI operational system and the mechanics of their movements. Each powered item had been equipped with the protections needed against EMP attacks. This place is amazing" I whispered through a cupped hand to Enah 2 (E 2).

"I am glad to see all of the items I am use to using and the new ones you can help me understand and use. So I will be in need of your help. Thank you for your offer," I said looking around and then at Hasenaty (Hans) (the horse), "I think with your guidance we can get your back legs working again."

Hasenaty (Hans) went over to one of the lower work tables and managed to climb up on it and laid down.

"Open the lower panel on the inside of my upper left thigh and now look for the red connector with three wires running from it," he instructed.

"Yes, I see them," I said.

"Disconnect them by pinching both sides and pulling straight up on the red connector at the same time. These are the live wires that connect my left back leg to the main power unit. Now push on the upper panel of the same hip, this area will open and show the mechanics to this leg," he said while looking at the view screen overhead.

From where the cameras were place he could see everything I was doing.

After opening the next panel I could see things that looked out of place and my machine logic set in and I informed him of what I thought the problem was.

"Yes, please replace the smaller rod and then reset the timing and stroke length," he agreed. "You will find the smaller rod in the third drawer of the second silver chest, on that table," he said using his nose to point in that direction.

After replacing the small rod he was able to move the one leg but not the ankle. He lifted the leg into the air and I heard a rolling sound, ever so faint.

"Oh my, I'm heard a faint rolling when you lifted your leg. It sounded like a nut or a bolt," I informed him.

"Yes and I felt it," he said.

I opened the upper thigh panel again and the nut had rolled to where I could see it. I grabbed the proper tool and got it out. "Here is the loose piece," I said holding it where Hasenaty (Hans) could see it.

"Oh, yes that is the reason my ankle wouldn't bend. You will need to close the present panel and open the one on my lower inside ankle. There I am sure you will find the problem," he coached.

"Yes, I see the problem. The bolt is pretty much still in place. It just needs a small adjustment and the nut replaced," I said.

"Good, aw yes. You have it right. Now you can connect the red plug so I can have full movement in that leg. I believe we make a good team," he said with a slight whinny type laugh.

After Hasenaty (Hans) was working in fine order and he had full use of all four legs we were off to gather Rumo's other pets that needed help. The musolot (cat) seemed to be able to move alright and only needed a few small adjustments with his ears. He complained about not being able to turn them to hear better and one eye was lazy.

The nisomite (dog) came wondering into the operation's unit just as we were finishing the adjustments on the musolot (cat) whose name turned out to be Monostad (Stan).

The nisomite's (dog) name was Likamo (Lika). He was having trouble curling his tail. After getting him on the exam table I had to open several small panels on his tail to find the problem. Seems one of the small cable lines had snapped and recoiled around a few other parts. Hasenaty (Hans) suggested cleaning up the mess and splicing the old cable back together. I decided to put in a new cable. My thought was that a splice may get hung up and snagged again.

"Wow! It feels so good to be able to curl my tail again," Likamo (Lika) said with a slight yip afterwards as he ran out of the door.

I do think that Rumo is sending the animals to the operation's unit because Likamo (Lika) just got through the door and the solaka (monkey) came in and was complaining of a rip in one ear and he couldn't hear in the other one.

"Ah, Roppuk (Rob) (the monkey), jump

up here on this exam table and let Nekuma (Nick) and me take a look at you," Hasenaty (Hans) said standing by one of the higher exam tables.

"I can stitch the one ear, but the hearing problem may take an operation. Are you up for an operation?" I asked.

"Yes! Please, I need to be able to hear with both ears. Please do it for me," he pleaded.

"Ok lie down on the table on your side so that the ear with the hearing problem is up," I instructed.

Hasenaty (Hans) spoke up, "You need to open the small panels behind the ear on the side of his head next to his ear," sort of pointing with his front hoof.

After opening the panels, I turned to look at Hasenaty (Hans) to give an unspoken question as to what next.

"Disconnect the green wire. This will kill the power unit to that ear. It needs to be checked to see if it is working right," he offered as a reply to my silent query.

"The power unit checks out to be working fine. Now what?" I asked.

"Leave it disconnected for now. You will need to detach the outer ear, and open the panels around the ear base. Then push the small purple button in the second panel while holding down the blue button in the first panel," he informed me.

I did as instructed and the whole ear

core popped out of his head.

"Oh. This makes it much easier to do repairs," I said looking closer at it. "I see the problem; there is a small blue spider shaped piece with wires for legs. It looks a little damaged."

"They are in the fifth drawer of the second cabinet on that wall," Hasenaty (Hans) said pointing in the direction with his nose.

"I need the blue one. I'm only finding the yellow ones," I said sort of raising my voice to be heard.

"Oh! Sorry. Try in the sixth drawer," he replied.

"Oh good, here they are," I said.

We got Roppuk (Rob)'s (the monkey) ear put back together and I stitch and glued his other ear.

"Ok! You are all done," I said, "How are you felling?"

"Good. Really good, I can hear out of both ears real good now. Thank you, Roppuk (Rob) said offering me his hand.

We touched hands and he left.

After Roppuk (Rob) left there was a few minutes of peace and quiet. This gave us enough time to straighten up the operation's unit. Just as we finished Rumo's bodrooka (raccoon) came scampering through the door and hopped up on one of the shorter exam tables, ran to the end of it and made a leap to one of the taller ones. He stood up on his back legs and introduced himself.

"My name is Gerset (Gar) (the raccoon), I am here to have repairs done," he said and then sat down.

It seemed his complaint was first about three broken toes on his back left foot and he had lost his night vision. I knew the broken toes were pretty much easy to fix, but the night vision I figured I may need help with. So I looked over at Hasenaty (Hans) to see if he knew about eyes and night vision. He gave me a nod.

"Ok, come over here and sit closer and let me see your foot," I said patting the table closest to where I was standing.

Working on feet and hands was one of the easier repairs because the outer layer came off like a glove or stocking. You just had to know where to press and what panel to open or the right buttons to push.

"Ok. How do your toes feel now? Wiggle them for me please, before I replace the padded foot layer," I requested "Good they look like they are working fine." I continued.

"Yes, they feel great. It feels good to be able to move them and grip things again," Gerset (Gar) (the raccoon) said gripping a pencil that had been lying on the table next to him.

"Ok, for the next part, dealing with your eyes, I will be needing you to lay down," I informed him.

I then took a good light and my magnaglasses and took a look into the back part of his eyes. That area looked ok, so I figured the problem must me in one or more of the components. I placed what I was seeing on the viewer so that Hasenaty (Hans) could see it as well.

"Let's move on to the other components, this area looks ok," he said.

"I agree. So what needs to be done to open the next area?" I asked

"Look in the temple area, first on the left. Then we can look at the right side. You will find one tuft of hair that is a little longer than the rest. Lift up on it, away from the side of the head. Then there should be an orange button with brown tones. Push it, and the eye should pop out like the ear did on Roppuk (Rob) (the monkey)," Hasenaty (Hans) explained.

"Ok. That sounds easy enough," I said finding and pulling the tuft of hair. Under the tuft right in plain sight was the button that Hasenaty (Hans) told me about and I pushed it like I was told. Sure enough the whole eye came sliding out on what looked like a tray. All of the components were right there, just offering themselves to be tested.

"Now use the systcal to check the entire components and circuit system one at a time. We need to find the one that is at fault for the night vision not working," Hasenaty (Hans) explained.

I was glad that Hasenaty (Hans) could talk telepathically to just one person at a time.

But I guess I looked a little confused. When he said systcal, I wasn't at all sure what he was referring to.

He laughed with a slight whinny. "You will find the systcal on the bottom shelf of the thirst cabinet on your left. It is the one that looks like half of a ball with red stripes.

I took it out and placed it near Gerset (Gar) head to keep it handy.

"Open the top half of the systcal and plug in the green wire to the front of it. Now place the other end of the green wires on the purple connections and switch the dial to zero. Tell me what the reading says," Hasenaty (Hans) requested.

"I am getting a two. Is that good or bad?" I ask.

"It's ok but not as good as it should be. Put the green wires on the orange wires now and tell me what you get," he instructed.

"I'm getting a twelve on the orange," I said.

"Good that is what we want. Now try the green wires on the yellow leads and let me know," he said.

"I'm getting a ten on the yellow leads," I informed him.

Now try them on the green one and then the blue wires," he requested.

"Well I got four on the green ones and ten on the blue ones," I said. *"I have tried the green wires on all of the leads I see. What is the verdict?"* I asked.

"Looks like the green and purple

components need to be changed out. I think those are the ones that are causing the night vision problems. At least in the left eye, we will need to do the same test in the right eye," he explained.

"You will find the green and purple components in the same cabinet you got the systcal from but they will be in one of the six drawers." Hasenaty (Hans) instructed.

After putting Gerset (Gar)'s eye back into place and closing the opening near his ear. I had him check his vision in his left eye. And we got positive results so I went to work on his right eye and before long Gerest was ready for the night life again. When he left we chattered happily all the way down the hall.

"Well that takes care of all of Rumo's pet. Now you have the larger animals to deal with. But I will be with you the whole time. They all know me, so there won't be any problems doing the repairs. I have the list of repairs that is needed to be done. That list was downloaded into my memory banks just after Rumo put in the request for you to come," Hasenaty (Hans) explained.

After all of the repairs were taken care of it was time for the evening meal and then time to sleep. I dozed off and woke up in the Time chamber.

I pulled off the helmet quickly. I had a few questions I really needed to have answered to.

"Enah 2 (E 2), I am a little confused as to all that I just seen and did. I had remembered part of this before my trip this time. But isn't Saturn considered a gas giant now? What happened? Does anyone know?" I asked.

"Yes, the time you just visited was in Saturn's early history before the larger wars took place, before it had rings. They nearly blew the planet apart with all of the explosives they used. No one can live there now. There are a few colonies on one of the moons yet," he explained.

"Thank you for letting me know this. Is this all the trips we have time for this sestron (today)?" I asked.

"Yes, I think we will work in another area of space tostron (tomorrow). But that is it for this sestron (day). Thank you Elaytay (Tay), see you in the amacron (morning)," he said.

"Okay, good ponacron (evening) Enah 2 (E 2)," I said as I headed for the door and then home.

Chapter Five
Psy Power

"Good amacron (morning) Enah 2 (E 2). Sorry I think I am a little late," I said walking through the doors into the science lab.

"No just in time. We had a few things to do before you got here this amacron (morning)," he said with a smile. "We are about ready to start," he added.

"Any idea where or when I am headed this amacron (morning)?" I asked.

I think the time is back when most of Strong Bow's planet's land masses were still together. Back before they made the split," he offered showing me a picture of "Mother" as Papa Two Wolves called it (Earth).

"What kind of people am I meeting? Do we know much about them?" I asked.

"All I have written here is that the people that called themselves the Lamurs were on a land mass separated by a large gulf from those who called themselves Atlants.

The Lamurs believed in working with nature and using physical labor along with the psychic powers of their minds in unison with nature. And the Atlants needed instant gratification in everything they did and seemed to not like physical labor. They had created other beings through DNA and genetic manipulations to do all of the physical duties of life for them. This is not to say that they didn't like looking perfect in their own standards but physical changes was all done with machines. So very little if any patience was used in their lives," he explained. "But I am not sure which of the two you will be visiting," he added.

I went in and put on my helmet, laid back and took a few long deep breaths to relaxed, knowing I would soon be among one of the two societies.

"I'm standing alone in a nicely groomed grove of apple trees, or at least that is what they look like. I am seeing a few other beings in a distance that seem to be working on the plants. Their physical bodies seem to fit the jobs they are doing.

I'm dressed in a light weight soft tunic that is nearly to the ground. I can hear a stream nearby, so I am going to go see who I am or if I can be seen," I said aloud but under my breath as not to be heard by anyone who happens to be near that I hadn't seen. "Oh! I may be first person. I just found a basket with a few flowers near my feet," I added.

"Sister Malona," came a voice from behind me.

As I turned I saw a young man that was dressed in what looked to be a special robe and attached to his chest was a rather large square plaque of gold mixed with silver, copper and nickel with precious gem stone aliened in a special design. My first thought is that he is the priest from a nearby temple. I'm still not completely sure what part I play in this society. My mind seems to be clear and my energy is high, but usually when I bounce in as one of the live people I have a dream like memory to build on. But I like to check and make sure it is a true memory before completely acting on it. I feel I'm in an area of the planet that needs care, and it is being abused.

"Oh, hello Father Rysal (Ray)," I said greeting him with a smile. His name came easy but I'm still not real sure as to what is going on or the part I play.

"Taking a little break between

sessions I see," he said.

"Yes, we take turns sitting in the high seat," I answered easily.

"I too, am taking a rest while on my way to talk with Sir Ralstant about an urgent matter.

"Peace be with you." I said with a slight bow with hands together in front of my face. And with a slight nod he walked on.

"It seems that I am one of the twelve priestesses that help with the foretelling of future happenings. Not that it made much of a difference to those who came in for a reading. To most it was like getting a suggestion note in a mail box. On the other hand the messages were recorded and secretly sent to the Lamurs, who did hear them and made the appropriate change in their lives.

The people I am dealing with here do insist on instant gratification and didn't want to change their way of life. They love pushing buttons and instantly having anything they desire. I know some are getting head gear that amplifies their thoughts so all they have to do is say what they want and it is there, being created out of thin air. For instance if one wants a glass of water, just hold out their hand as if they are being handed a glass and say it, and it appears in their hand. Do they not know, that this cannot go on forever? Those atoms and molecules have to come from somewhere?" I said quietly under my breath for Enah 2 (E 2) to hear. "I never made it to the stream. Don't think it is needed right away since I can clearly be seen and I'm a part of this time. I'm making my way back to the temple area. This will give me a closer look at the city, at least part of it. I am taking a little different way back.

I just passed a very tall building with emerald green windows and silver trim in the shape of a large pyramid. There are a few very odd shaped building with strange decorations on them. If I am remembering right that is one of the main science experimental labs.

Walking towards me is a Centaur. His back is loaded down with bundles and he has more in his arms. As I get closer to him he has stopped, and standing very still. Now he is give a deep bow to me.

I gave him a smile and walked on. Others in front of me have passed him and he didn't react at all. I have seen a few others, like a bird person flying overhead with bundles hanging from around his neck and a long tube held in one foot. I've seen cross bred humanoids created for certain jobs in the meadows, fields and I imagine they are working in the water and forest too. I am remembering from the past now that some have sought me out to tell me their stories. Some of them, maybe I should say most of them have been created to help in time of war. But some of them have gotten away and have learned to survive and multiply as a new life form. All of them that I have met are very smart and care very much for the planet they live on.

I am nearing the temple and it is beautiful, it seems made of very brightly polished alabaster with gold trimmed steps. The front entry gate is made of thin sheets of quartz crystal held together with copper, nickel and silver strips.

'Inside is a vast array of very large crystals of all kinds and colors. I know how to gather their energy and work with it. I put on a silken veil over my head and breast plate of special gems and walk to the golden room and now sitting on a large crystal chair the middle of the room. I am handed something very sweet to drink. I take a small sip and"… 'going into a deep trance. I can see things as if I am watching a telelink (TV screen). I am to tell the person standing quietly in front of me what I have seen. Part of it is a warning to this person and part of it can be their future. I let them know and the priest collects funds and hurries them out. This goes on for a few more decons (hours), and when I get a break I get a chance to secretly pass the info to a friend, who in turn makes sure it gets to the right sources for the Lamurs and send the word back to them as to what to expect.'

"I am hoping that you are able to see all that I have seen. Have you?" I asked Enah 2 (E 2) in an almost silent whisper.

"Yes I can see all that you have seen and heard most of it. Except for the visions, you can tell us about them when you get back." He said.

"This abuse of reforming molecules out of the air into what they desire at the moment has gone on far too long with the people of Atlantis just taking what they want without putting anything back. I don't think they really pay attention to anything I and the four others tell them. They come and get their readings but then go about their lives as if we say nothing. I have told them that they can't keep using the planet's creative energy to make things appear just because they are too lazy to get up and go get what they want, but they are not listening. Soon, very soon things will have to give and I don't think they will like the results. I know deep in my heart that this area of the planet can't take much more abuse." I told one of my sister priestess.

'There are a few Lamurs working throughout the city and surrounding areas and they all know the escape routes to get out of the city fast. There have already been a few sink holes that the scientist couldn't explain. That is the start and it is up to me and a few others to get the warning out quick enough to give all time to run to safe areas.'

'A lot of the Centaurs have managed to leave along with a few of the other life forms that were created here. I am in touch with the merpefish (mermaids and mermen) and others who give me telepathic information. The time is getting ever closer each day and I feel danger will strike very soon. I only sleep for about three hours at a time because the people of Atlantis never seem to sleep. There is always someone who is asking a question from one of the five of us.'

'I was just handed a special shell and was told that only the telepaths can hear it and it is to be sounded as the warning. I took it and gave thanks to the being that gave it to me. I had never seen such a being before. He was almost glowing so brightly it was hard to look at him. I was told to sound it in three days at

time the sun is straight above me. I agreed
and bowed, when I stood up he was gone
but I'm not sure where he went. There was
nothing near me that would hide him.'

"I hope you are able to gather all of
my thoughts. Because I can't talk out loud
in very many places without gathering
attention I don't need," I said, hoping that
Enah 2 (E 2) heard me.

"Yes we are gathering the thought
they are coming through real clear. Not to
worry," he replied.

"Good," I said feeling relieved.

Days passed and it was time. I
sounded the shell and all telepaths excused
themselves from their jobs and left. Some
using passageways that were made for
them while others when over land, but all
of them in the same direction toward the
high point behind the high temple. Those of
us in the temple had a secret passage to
leave by. The merpeople (mermaids and
mermen) all swam away from the continent
to be safer. And as we all stood on the safe
spot we were told to go to, the land masses
were dividing and a great body of water
filled in where Atlants was. We watched
the continent slowly crumble as if to fall
into a very large sink hole and the water
filled it..

As the last of it went under I found

myself back in the science time chamber.

But I was remembering even more information about the things that were happening there than I had time to pass on at the time.

"That was a very strange visit I said," looking up a Enah 2 (E 2) as he took the helmet off of me.

"Yes I have to agree," he said. "But you know that is one of the Universal laws, when you borrow from one place it needs to be replaced. Nature hates a void," he said nodding his head to make the point.

"But it wasn't only that. I mean the part about using artificial means to make things out of nothing by taking atoms from other places. They were doing experiments on DNA and mutations of human, animals and plants. Some of the humanoids for the lack of a better term were very intelligent. And in some ways were more so than the scientist that came up with the ideas. I mean they had more of what we call common sense that their creators. I think that was the biggest downfall. Their creators didn't think things out before acting on them. A lot of their creations got away from them and escaped the sinking. Some of them weren't so different from some of the peoples we have found on other planets. All of them had talents of their own and loved life and were very open minded when it came to others and life. I am finding that for us as two legged humanoids, to think we are so much better or smarter, than any living thing that doesn't look the same as us or talk different is just really dumb on our part," I said feeling I needed to voice my opinion. "While I was there, I did find out that some of the changes they had made to the humans and animals on land were made for the benefits of war. And the ones that were made to live in the water was made for labor and experimental ways to live underwater. They had some of the merpeople setting up generators to turn the ocean currents into energy. I can see where there may be benefits in that but at the same time they weren't taking safety precautions to protect the other animals in the ocean." I added.

"I think you may be proven right," Enah 2 (E 2) said with a smile.

"You know there was such a difference between the Atlantas and the Lamurs. They were like a world apart." I said, thinking about the trip.

"Well they were from different planets, and if I remember the stories right. The Atlantas invaded the Lamurs' planet and they didn't want to fight so they took everyone that wanted to leave and found another place to live. But the Atlantas followed them again after all of the resources were used up on the planet they took over from the Lamurs. This kind of thing was common before the United Planet's Alliance was formed to keep things a little more fair for all involved.

Do we have time for another adventure this sestron (day)," I asked.

"No I think we should call it a sestron (day)," he said.

"Okay, see you in the amacron (morning) then. Bye," I said with a wave as I walked through the doors.

Chapter Six
Planet of Wee Folk

"Good amacron (morning) Enah 2 (E 2). Where am I off to this sestron (day)?" I asked as I walked through the doors of the science time lab.

"We got word last ponacron (evening) that this sestron (day) we are to send you back in time, to a small planet that found itself in the middle of two warring planets and was blasted into fragments," he said pointing at a star map. "We know that area as the asteroid belt." He added

"What happen to the people that lived on it?" I asked looking at the map.

"We aren't really sure. There are stories of people who have seen them on other planets. But those stories haven't been proven. That is where you come in. You are to find out as much as you can about all of the peoples in the short time you will be there. I don't think it will take more than a few pestrons (weeks) at most," he said looking at his timelink (like a watch).

"Okay then we should get started. Everything has been checked, right?" I asked referring to our time travel equipment's check list.

"All checked and ready to go," came the answer from one of the techs.

"Oh! And that few pestrons (weeks) is their time, Right!" I asked looking over my shoulder at Enah 2 (E 2).

"Yes," he said with a big smile.

"Good," I said while sitting down in the chair and putting on the helmet. "Now to relax," I added while slowing my breathing.

I drifted off, completely relaxed and next thing I knew, I was opening my eyes to a totally new environment. There was thick vegetation everywhere I looked. The leaves were very large and the trees were huge. Everything in this place was oversized.

I found a small puddle of water and looked in it. "This is strange Enah 2 (E 2). I look like myself and I have on a helmet that is almost visible. Am I really here," I asked, hoping to get an answer quickly.

Just as I was looking around one of the leaves rustled in back of me. I spun around to find what I had only seen drawings of. I think they are called fairies. 'Oh my gosh. This is where they came from?' I thought while standing face to face with one. The surprising thing is, he is the same size as me or is it the other way around?'

"Yes, this is our home planet and yes I can hear your thought. How did you hear about us?" he asked with his hand on his hips and his wings folded together and standing straight out behind him.

"Sorry. My name is Elaytay (Tay) and I was sent here to learn as much as I can about all of the peoples on this planet," I said, wanting to be truthful, hoping that he would be willing to help me.

"You seem the friendly sort. I don't think that the council will have a problem with you meeting others here," he answered.

"By the way I am known as Lintus (Lin)," he added with a smile.

As we walked along a small path he explained why everything looked so large to me. It seems that when I got to this planet, I had been made the average size of most of the beings that live here.

"So where are you from and why are you curious about the beings on this planet," he asked point blank.

"Well, I guess I may as well tell you

the whole story. I am what is known as a time traveler on my planet and I have come here to learn as much as I can about everyone who lives here," I said hoping he would still be willing to help me.

"Okay. Well number one thing to know about our planet, is that most all of the being that live on it are willing to share. You will find that most of us are curious about visitors who happen to just drop by," he said with a hardy laugh. "I am known as a fairy. That is a species name. There are many clans/kinds of fairies with many different powers and gifts. We all have special skills and jobs we do to help other growing things in our world.

As we walked into the center of their village, we were met by all kinds of fairies. Some had wings and some didn't. There were some with bright colors and some of duller colors that blended in with the plants and animals because of the marking that help them to never be seen. There were all sizes and shapes. Some had antenna and the shapes of their faces differed from each other so it was easy to tell who was who.

Then one dressed in a long silken robe stepped forward. "You must be our visitor that Lintus (Lin) set the message about.

E lay tay (Tay)? Is it? And you are what

your people call a time traveler?" she asked putting her hand out toward me as a greeting.

"Yes, I am. And thank you for meeting me," I said placing my hand into hers.

"My name is Anreauna (Ann)," she said, "I am head council member of our area," she added.

"You will find we are very easy to get along with, this is not to say that we do have a few here and there that are a little hard to get along with. Some of us think it is because they don't feel good, had a bad day or maybe have allergies," she said with a giggle. "We get along the best one can with those who see life a little different than we do," she added.

"This is Addeus (De), he will be glad to show you around and answer most of your questions," she said putting her hand out toward Addeus (De).

Addeus (De) bowed very deeply and presented me with a very large smile.

"Thank you Addeus (De), glad to meet you. What will you show me first?" I asked as we walked farther into town.

"We'll stop here while you let your people know what is happening," he said, stopping to look straight at me. "Yes we know of your contacts and their needs. You see we are sort of traveler too" he continued.

"Thank you," I said.

"I am a little confused with my travels here. I am not just an observer, or using another life's name as usual. Or is it that I am using a name that has been repeated," I asked hoping to get an answer from Enah 2 (E 2).

"It could be that you were known there as Elaytay (Tay) or that time for this planet is not the same time as for us. I am not sure of this and have no answer for you," Enah 2 (E 2) said in a puzzled tone.

"Maybe I can help you a little with this," Addeus (De) said with a smile. "You see time for us and everyone on this planet; time works a little differently than it does other places. We are not fixed in one realm or dimension as you understand it," he continued.

"Oh well, that explains a lot. Thank you," I said, breathing a little easier.

"You see we can and are able to transverse time with ease. We, that is a lot of our kind, has learned to transcend time and space in a moments flash. That is not to say that some have taken one a slightly heavier life existence and prefer to stay in one realm and have regular lives with the birth and death experiences. These can still travel to other realms but their lives are anchored in only one," he explained.

"Are there others who have transcended time like you have?" I asked.

"Yes, there are a few others that started on the denser realms and have managed to move their expression of life to these lighter realms. This was taught to all from the beginning of life, but few have really heard what was being taught. Most just think they are nice stories and pass them off as stories," he added.

"Wow. I think I have heard some of those stories but didn't really take much notice of them because I was told they were nice stories, and great tales of magic," I said, thinking back on some of the stories I had been told about great teachers who taught meditations and other things.

"So show me more of what is here," I said eager to see as much as I could in the time I was given.

Just then he waved his hand and in front of us was a heavy fog like area and in that fog was like a view screen. "Well as you can see" he said holding out an open hand toward the view, "We have villages and we live pretty much the same as other life forms throughout the Universes. Which I must add there are plenty of." Just then the view switched to what looked to be outer space and I could see all of the different Galaxies and Universes. They seemed to be endless. "In fact it would take a few of your life times to count all of them," he said while holding out his hand as display toward their village as the fog cleared.

"Wow that is great. I wouldn't have thought there were that many planets," I said sort of surprised. I knew there was a lot but didn't really realize there were that many.

I looked a little closer at the village and the peoples in it. There were some going in and out of shops and one was planting seeds and watering them. One was feeding animals, 'I think they may be pets'.

"Yes, those are Glen's pets. He loves caring for the animals in our area. And as you can see we make the things we need. We don't believe in just taking materials out of the air and instantly creating what we need, unless it is an emergency and then they are put back when the dilemma is over, otherwise it makes things imbalanced," he explained. "We have what you would know as farmers, builders, repair persons and others to make anything we need or use," he continued.

Just then I saw a family playing with their two children in a park like area.

"Oh, I see you spotted a family. We live in mixed realms or dimensions. There are a few that can cross and some that have chosen to stay on just one," he explained.

"What other beings live on this planet?" I asked.

"Oh, we have a lot of different beings that share this world but not all realms like my group does. Come I will take you one a tour," he said as we walked up the side of a tall hill.

At the top I could see what looked like steps leading to nowhere. 'Wonder what those are for?'

"Come on and I will show you what those stairs are for," he said.

I had forgotten that he could read my thoughts.

"Okay," I said with a grin, feeling a little embarrassed.

He ran to the top of the stairs, took out a whistle and blew it. I could barely hear any sound from it. But I did hear a rush of wings getting closer to where we were standing, now that I had made it to the top step. I looked around to see a peg-acorn landing and trotting up to where we were standing. She's a beautiful unicorn with a golden horn protruding from the middle of her forehead and the most beautiful feathered wings. 'I hope you are getting all of this Enah 2 (E 2).'

"This is Montonanol (Monty), she will be taking us to see things," he said turning to introduce her.

"Where would you like for me to take you Master Addeus (De)?" Montonanol (Monty) asked looking back at us as we climbed onto her back and strapped into the small seats strapped to a waist band.

"Oh just fly us around. I want Elaytay (Tay) to be able to see the different beings that live on this planet," he instructed.

"Of course, as you wish," she said as she started to run.

She only ran a short distance before her great wings caught the air and we lifted off the ground and gain speed. Then she dipped and I could see what I thought may have been giants.

"Were those giants? And are they mean like the ones I have heard tales of?" I asked.

"No the ones that you have heard tales of are the ones that are caught in just one realm because of their anger at the warring planets that soon cause the destruction of this one. These are the ones that can live where ever they choose at the time," he explained.

Then Montonanol (Monty) flew higher into the cloud and then made another dip. Addeus (De) took out a flute and played a simple few notes and I had a chance to see what I had been told were the tree spirits. The beings that live in and among the trees, some of the names I remembered was wood nymphs or dryads, devany, faunis, gubilly, ganes, hildermod, lunantesh and gnomes. It seems they had all heard the flute and made themselves seen by waving as we flew over. I waved back and got a few smiles and cheers.

"This is great," I said looking over at Addeus (De).

He played a few more notes and we took a sharp turn to the right I could see we were getting closer to streams, lakes and larger rivers and out in the far distance I could see what may even be an ocean. Addeus (De) took up the flute again as we passed over the bodies of water and blew a long steady blend of two notes. I looked behind us as we flew towards the large body of water and I could see all sizes of ripples in the waters we had just passed. As I turned around to see where we were, I could see that the larger body of water was like our oceans. And as we made a large circular turn to the left I could see merpeople, Silkes, and Oceanids coming to the surface and waving with large smiles and some even started to sing. Then we started to approach the land with its rivers, streams and lakes. I could see a few strange animals like the hubsin along with devany, fossagrins, annun, lorela, naids, buccas, undines and a gruadach with a gentle hand on one of the animals. Some of them were in the water and some were at the shallows or water's edge but all were waving a greeting in my direction.

Just then we made an upward sweep high about the clouds and there off in the distance I could see other winged beings. Some of their feathers were full of brilliant colors; some seemed to have long trails flowing behind them as we got closes Addeus (De) started to name them.

"The silfs are the ones with dark to light blues. The tangu have the yellows and the hypersprites have the green to fire oranges while the mazikin have more of the purples," he explained.

Just then one flew by that looked like it had a human face. I had to turn and look again and as I turn back to ask Addeus (De) what.

He answered with a laugh. "That is what we call Jimano (Jim). He and his group loves showing off," he chuckled.

"Oh," I said taking a deep breath of relief.

"Hold on we are headed for the larger groups," he said just as Montonanol (Monty) took a dive to get below the clouds.

"Ooooh!" I shouted just as we leveled off and flew over a few very tall mountains where I had a chance to see a few other kinds of strange beings and one jumps and waved that looked a lot like my friend Notnah (Not) but he was all white.

As I looked up we were flying in closer to what looked like large stone houses. Montonanol (Monty) slowed her flight and slowly landed trotting to a stop near another set of stairs like the ones we climbed to take this ride.

"This place is very large. Who lives here?" I asked turning to Addeus (De).

"This is my good friend Ashurit (Ash). He and his family live here and the rest of their village is on the other side of that hill," he explained while pointing to the east.

About that time Ashurit (Ash) came walking out of his house.

"Glad you could make it," came his booming voice out of the quietness.

I guess I sort of made a wrinkle in my face because of the loudness. It almost hurt my ears.

"Oh sorry, I forget that you're a lot

smaller than I and I need to use a softer voice than I do with my other friends," he said holding out his hand to the top of the stairs.

Addeus (De) climbed onto his hand and motioned for me to follow. I followed and soon we were placed in his vest pocket. It was shallow enough that standing the edge came almost at armpit height. It felt safe and Addeus (De) gave me a nod to let me know that everything is okay.

Ashurit (Ash) took us into his house and placed us on the table, where his wife soon brought us a small plate with apple pieces cut just the right size for us to eat with ease.

"So what are you doing on my side of the mountain today," he asked looking at Addeus (De).

"I was showing Elaytay (Tay) our planet and all of the beings on it. We flew over the forest and water ways and ocean and thought we would stop by to see you on our way to see the rest," Addeus (De) explained.

"So you are Elaytay (Tay). I had heard we had a visitor and if I heard right, you are a time traveler?" he asked while sitting down nearby so he would be as low as we were.

"Yes, I was sent to find out more

about your planet and the beings that lived here," I said while reaching for another piece of apple.

"You say lived here," what do you mean by the past tense of lived," he said looking a little concerned.

"Well, I would need to check with my people about that statement before I could explain it more. So if you wouldn't mind waiting for a few moment while I check in with them? Please?" I answered knowing that I needed more information before saying anything else.

"Yes of course, you can use that end of the table," Ashurit (Ash) said as he pointed a finger.

"Enah 2 (E 2), you heard the question. What should I tell them?" I asked.

"I am sure that Addeus (De) knows already but you may want to know if he is able to see the future before you say much more," Enah 2 (E 2) replied.

I could feel that I had gotten myself in a sort of sticky situation and I wasn't really sure how to handle it. I was going to have to rely on my intuition to help me out.

"Addeus (De), Can you come here so I can talk to you. Please?" I asked.

"I have a few questions and need a few answers before I answer Ashurit (Ash)'s question. How tall are we?" I asked to see if my hunch was right.

"I would say about six inches in you measuring units," Addeus (De) answered with a questioned look on his face.

"And since you can travel into other realms and see things in time, have you seen what happened to this planet in the future?" I asked, needing to see if he already knew the future of this planet.

"Yes I have. And I think I know where you are going with your questions. I have seen the destruction of this planet but it is a long time from now and not to worry Ashurit (Ash) and his family will not be here when all of that happens. In fact most of the beings here are finding other place to live already. But you see most of us will not need a mode of travel because we can just think of where we want to be and we are there. Ashurit (Ash) and his family will be off planet at the time it is taken out of being," he said, looking at me as if to ask if he was right in knowing.

"Yes, that is part of it. But I was also wondering how tall Ashurit (Ash) is," I asked.

"I would say about the same size as the average men on your planet," he said.

I started laughing. "I was thinking at first that he was a giant and then I got to thinking that I was just smaller than I was used to being," I said trying not to laugh to loud.

Ashurit (Ash) tapped the table with his fingers to get our attention, which rattled the board under our feet. As we turned to look at him, he asked. "What is funny, I like to laugh too,"

"Nothing really that funny," Addeus (De) explained. "Elaytay (Tay) was wondering if you were what her people would call a giant. And I told her no, that you were normal size, she was just smaller than usual," he continued with a chuckle.

"Now what about then past tense you used a few moments ago," Ashurit (Ash) asked.

"Well maybe I had better explain that. She was sent to learn as much as she can about all of us. Some of us may move to other places and some may not live forever," Addeus (De) explained. "Does that answer the past tense for you?" he asked.

"Yes, thank you. That puts my mind at ease. At first I thought maybe something was going to happen to us with all of the space wars that are going on right now," Ashurit (Ash) said, breathing easier now.

"It was nice to be here with you Ashurit (Ash) and thank you for the treat. We enjoyed your company and our visit, but we are off the see the desert where it meets the seas," Addeus (De) said with a bow. "Now if you wouldn't mind taking us back out so we can catch a ride with Montonanol (Monty).

"Not at all," Ashurit (Ash) said as he gently picked us up and placed us back in his vest pocket for the ride back out to where we were to catch our ride. "Hope to see you again soon. Nice to meet you Elaytay (Tay)," he said giving me a nod.

"Nice to meet you, Ashurit (Ash)," I said with a bow as Addeus (De) took out his flute and gave a couple of tones.

It wasn't long before we could hear the beating of large wings up on the late afternoon winds. Montonanol (Monty) landed with a thud and came totting up as proud as if she had made the best landing ever.

"Off to the desert where it meets the seas, Montonanol (Monty)," Addeus (De) said as we strapped into our seats.

She looked back over her shoulder and gave a whinny as if to approve. And we lifted off with a clatter of hooves and the beating of her large wings.

After flying for a little while I could see the deserts off in the far distance. Just then a large gust of wind hit Montonanol (Monty) square and set her off balance. We had been high enough that her ears were in the clouds. But now we were tumbling towards the planet out of control. Then she was flipped completely upside down and Addeus (De) was out of his seat and dangling by just the one strap he managed to grab as his harness broke. I reached out for him but couldn't touch his hands, but he held out his flute towards me to grab and I did. It slipped from his hand.

"Play it," he shouted. "Play A,C,E and B flat," he shouted over the howling winds.

"I don't know how to play the flute," I said.

"Try to relax and not think about it. Just let your hands move. They will play the right notes," he encouraged.

I did as he asked and the winds stopped and Montonanol (Monty) was able to right herself and Addeus (De) was able to get back in his seat. At this point we were very close to the ground.

"Just in time I would say. Good Job Elaytay (Tay)!" Addeus (De) said.

Montonanol (Monty) whinnied her approval too.

"That was a wild ride," Addeus (De) added with a laugh.

"Wilder than I want to do again anytime soon," I said taking a deep breath.

Then we both laughed. The sun was getting a little lower in the sky now and the colors were beautiful. There was no limit to the colors being displayed, mixing with the streaks of cloud wisps, it was beyond words.

Coming at us out of the clouds above us now was a streak that at first looked like fire. But it whipped and dove and then made a sharp turn in order to pass us.

"What was that?" I asked turning to see where it went.

"Oh that is our fire dragon. At least that is what we call him. He doesn't really breathe fire but his colors show as if they were on fire this time of day. And he has a very long bright red and orange tongue that he likes to flutter in front as he dives toward you. It almost looks as if he was shooting flames at you.

On the way back to Addeus (De)'s village we passed over a few other land marks and I had a chance to wave a hello to a few other creatures/beings that I had been told were mythical. Also on the way back Addeus (De) hinted that his people knew when and how their planet would be destroyed because they could see into other timelines and they were all connected in one way or another.

Soon Montonanol (Monty) whinnied and started to slow her speed for our decent to the landing point. Then there was the gentle but loud thud as her hooves first touched down and the clattered along the stone landing point that held the stairs in place.

"I sent word ahead that you wanted to know more about the ending of this planet," Addeus (De) said with a smile.

I guess I gave him an odd look before I remembered. "Oh, I had forgotten that you were able to communicate telepathically with each other," I said with a giggle.

When we got to the last step and I looked up Anreauna (Ann) was standing there a few feet in front of me.

Hello Elaytay (Tay), we meet again. I was told you would like to know more about how things end on this planet," she said. "Come with me and I will tell you all that we have found out. So you and your people don't have to worry about anyone that lives here," she added.

Addeus (De) and I followed her back to the village and she took me to the Council Hall, where all of the information was kept.

Anreauna (Ann) walked over to what looked like a closet and opened the large doors. There was nothing in it, not even the rod for things to hang from. But there was a small box sitting on the floor in the center of the closet. Anreauna (Ann) flipped a switch on it and picked up a small object from her desk and sat down beside me.

All of a sudden there was a bright light that flashed from the open closet.

"Oh, sorry, Rubeus had been studying these finding earlier while adding newer information and didn't reset the drive. Give me a few seconds. Please," Anreauna (Ann) said while playing with the item she had in her hands. The bright light turned off.

I smiled and said, "Sure, not a problem."

Then there was a smaller flash of light and when I looked up there was a large 3D map of the universe. It showed all of the planets and systems that we knew were present at this time.

Addeus (De) walked over to the display and took a long pointing stick and touched their planet and it quivered for a few seconds.

"That is where you are right now and the larger planets of either side of us are at war with each other. They are of the mindset that because our planet is smaller there is no life here. I guess partly that is our fault. Because when they sent their explorers every being here hid from them," Anreauna (Ann) informed me.

"Why hide?" I asked.

"Well that is a story within itself," she said looking at Addeus (De).

I could tell they were talking but I wasn't sure about what. But I waited quietly to see if I would get to hear that story.

"Ok, well long ago some of the beings on this planet where seen, caught, on other planets in another dimension and used as slaves. They had to do the bidding of the ones who captured them. And they really didn't want that to happen again and we all agreed. So that is why we all hid," Anreauna (Ann) explained.

"Anyway to get back to what is happening now," Addeus (De) said with a smile.

"Yes, yes of course," Anreauna (Ann) agreed coming back from her thoughts.

"Well the planets on either side of us are at war as I said and we know that at least one of them have developed a way to control the meteors that come through this way. They can magnetically turn them in a way that makes them hit the other planet.

And it seems that we are in the line of fire at certain times during their rotation around the sun. According to what we have seen in the different time lines we finally get hit enough that it starts a chain reaction in the weather and our planets inner core. But the warning is slow enough that everyone living here is able to relocate. The Beings here have their own way of getting from place to place," Anreauna (Ann) explained.

"I am really glad to hear that," I said with a sigh of relief.

Just then this small being opened and entered the room through a smaller door that was in the lower half of the main door. She had light blue skin, dark eyes and light yellow hair. Her arms and legs seemed unusually shorter than any of the other beings I had seen. She had on a shirt and vest and the pants she wore was sort of a cross between a skirt and leggings.

"Oh, hello Lanora. What can I help you with?" Anreauna (Ann) said smiling at her and then looked over at me. "This is Lanora, she is a part of a group we call the Rubumps. We have had many groups merge and fall in love and their children sometimes don't look like either of the parents. Rubumps came about when Fairies and Gnomes have children. Now they are their own group. All of their children look like them. Although some are a little different, in that they show the ability of using some of the fairy talents and magic," she added.

"I don't want to be a bother but Grundanl (Grun) is having trouble with a few birds that are determined to eat our planting seed," Lanora said, nervously ringing her hands.

Anreauna (Ann) went to the other room and brought Roosceo (Roo) back into the room. "Can you please go with Lanora and see that Grundanl (Grun) gets the help he needs?"

"Of course, right away," Roosceo (Roo) said, walking out of the room with Lanora leading.

"So as you can see there have been new groups that have come about because of love. All of the being in our realm get along and respect each other and their differences. Some look strange to others but we all know that this difference is what makes our realm strong. There is no selfishness, greed, or jealousy aloud. We have had a few that thought they were better and deserved more than others in the long past, but they were dealt with in a more natural way," Anreauna (Ann) said. "And now I am wondering if we have answered all of your questions and the questions of your peoples?"

"Let me check. The way I am set up Enah 2 (E 2), is able to hear and see most if not all that I see and hear. Enah 2 (E 2) is our science and time travel team leader," I said trying to explain how things worked for me as I travel.

"Check in and see what he says," Anreauna (Ann) instructed.

"I have heard and seem much of what you have Elaytay (Tay) and I have no other questions that I can think of at this time," Enah 2 (E 2) said as I covered my right ear.

"No, He says he can't think of any other questions at this time. But may I ask if another question comes up can I come back to see you?" I asked.

"Of course, but you won't have to come here. We are on your home planet and others at the same time. You can talk to us there. If you have a question in your future, just sit quietly and ask the question in your mind and we will send you the answer. But beware we do have a few that like to play trick. So I would say ask the same question in several different ways to see if you get the same answer," she said laughing.

"Thank you very much for letting

me see all that I did of your world and letting me know that all of you are safe," I said with a bow.

I could feel myself fading from their view and as I opened my eyes Enah 2 (E 2) was taking my helmet off.

"That was great. Did you get to see all of the things I saw? And hear all that was said? But you know the strangest part is that I wasn't just an observer this time or playing the part of myself with a different name and look. I was me, I mean just me, and it seemed a little strange," I said looking up at Enah 2 (E 2).

"Yes that part was a little strange. But like Anreauna (Ann) say they live in several realm or dimensions and can see the future and I think they knew you were coming to see them before you even showed up there," Enah 2 (E 2) said as he stepped away so I could get out of the chair.

"I think you are right, but it was still a little strange talking to them physically even though they could read what I was thinking. Is this the only trip we are doing?" I asked

"Yes, I think that is it for this sestron (day). It took a little longer than some of the other trip you have taken. But we did get a lot of information about what happened to their planet. So have a great ponacron (evening) at home.

"Thanks, see you in the amacron (morning)," I said as I walked out the door.

On the way home my mind wondered though all of the things I had a chance to see and hear. I found myself walking fast and faster until I was almost running to get there faster. I wanted to be able to tell the whole family about what I had done this sestron (day).

Chapter Seven
Rules to Live by

"Good amacron (morning) Enah 2 (E 2)," I said as I walked through the doors of the time chamber.

"Ah, good morning Elaytay (Tay)," He said looking up from his work.

"Where or should I say when am I headed for this sestron (day)," I asked with a big grin, remembering a joke I had been told earlier.

"Do you remember an old legend of the ones called the first male and female, I think in some groups there were named Adam and Eve?" He asked.

"Yes, I think they were supposed to be the first people created on the Planet I know as Earth," I said.

"Yes and that is what we want to find out more about. I am pretty sure you will just be an observer on this trip," Enah 2 (E 2) said holding out his hand toward the chair and my helmet.

"Ok," I said while sitting down in the travel chair as he handed me my helmet.

I put on my helmet and laid back in the chair and started to relax. It seemed that I had no more than closed my eyes when I was suddenly aware of a large leaf brushing my arm as I almost fell down. I opened my eyes to the most beautiful place you could ever imagine. "There are fruit and nut trees of just about every description you could imagine and the most wonderful smelling flowers ever smelled. Their colors are bright and are the varied colors of the rainbow and they are in all shape and sizes." I reported to Enah 2 (E 2) as a whisper. I didn't want to disturb anything.

"Tell me more." He requested.

"The animals large and small were all getting along and playing together. I mean this is fantastic. The lions and larger felines' young are playing with the lambs while the adults are laying close by watching. The crocodile has a bunny hopping over him and a smaller cat playing with his tail. This is what I would have been glad to call paradise. All of the animals are getting along. It is amazing to see. There is no aggressive behavior from any of them." I added.

Just then there was a large burst of wind and there in front of me was a very large person with their back to me, dressed in a long white robe.

" A being just entered the area, I can't tell if it is a male or female. But this being was a lot taller than I am. I am going to say he, because his voice is loud and forceful." I whispered. "Can you hear what I hear and are the visuals coming through?" I asked.

"Yes, everything is good here." Enah 2 (E 2) related.

I'm going too leaned to one side and try to see who he was talking to. He is talking to a young man, I think in his mid-twenties. I think this may be the one the legends called Adam but I had always pictured him differently. He is about average height and weight with dark eyes and dark shoulder length hair and his skin was sort of a light rusty reddish brown.

"In this place there is all of the food you will need. The days and nights are neither too hot nor cold. There are plenty of things for you to do. And I have given you the job of taking care of my garden for me. Do you understand all that I have asked of you?" the being said.

"Yes and I am taking care of the plants and visiting with all of your animals.

They all hold good conversations. I enjoy their company." Adam answered.

"Are you happy Adam?" asked the being.

"Yes, I have plenty to eat and things to do, and the air is never too cold or hot," he said slowly then looking down at the ground.

"Yes, but you look and act as if you feel there is something you want. What would that be?" asked the being.

"I have the animals to keep me company and talk to. And we hold great conversations, but it doesn't seem to complete me. I feel there is an empty spot in the pit of my stomach. But I don't know what it is," Adam said trying to explain the best he knew how. "The animals have others of their kind to be with." he added under his breath.

"Come walk with me," the being said. "I think I know what it is that you need. But before I take care of this need; you will need instructions to live by. Up till now you only had one rule and that was not to touch the tree at the top of the highest hill." the being said as they walked.

He pulled out a scroll and as he unrolled it he read." You shall not do any harm. This is not just to the physical plant, animal, yourself, other beings or the earth that you are on. But this law expands past the physical, the mental, emotional, spiritual and all other areas of creation." the being said.

They are walking out of my hearing range and there is nothing for me to hide behind in order to follow them. But that law alone covers a lot of things." I whispered to Enah 2 (E 2).

I'm following as close as I dared to." I said.

'They walked along this path together and soon I could see what seemed to be a camp. It is a clearing with a few rocks to sit on and in one area I can see that the long grass has been cut and laid in crisscross layers about the size of a bed. There is no roof anywhere in this clearing. The bed is under a tree with thick branches. Everything is green and the colored flowers seemed almost like a painting. There all kinds of colors, shapes and sizes, then I noticed that there were more kinds fruit and nut trees growing around the clearing along with bunches of berries and vegetables growing in perfect orders. They are all so perfect, it is hard to believe.' I thought hoping Enah 2 (E 2) was picking up my thoughts too.

Adam sat down on one of the rocks and looked at the ground.

"Tell me what is troubling you," the being demanded.

"I know that there are animals I can talk to and they visit and we play games and some help me with the gardening. I enjoy their company, but I have noticed that each of them have friends that look like them. There is no other one that looks like me. I walk on two feet and do not fly. I can swim but do not breathe underwater like the water animals do. I think I would like to have another being to talk to. Someone that can feel the things I feel and understand the way I think. I feel I need someone that I can talk to and to help me figure out things. I have watched the animals in the evening when it is time to go to sleep and they have another of their kind to talk to and lay close to," Adam said shyly.

"Oh that is not a problem. I understand now what you need. Lay down and take a nap and I will be back," the being said.

Adam laid down and as he did, the being waved his hand and Adam fell sound asleep.

There was another large rush of wind and now there are three other tall beings that just showed up on the right side of me and joined the other one. They all look like they were from the same race.

They picked Adam up and vanished. The main one that had been talking to Adam looked in my direction as if he could see me, then he also vanished.

I have managed to find some water to see if I had a reflection. I can sort of see myself, but I am also transparent. This was a little confusing.

"Enah 2 (E 2) this is confusing, my reflection shows me to be sort of transparent but I can still be seen, just see through. What does that mean?" I asked.

"That mean you may be able to be seen so just stay out of sight," came the answer.

'Great. I need to learn all I can, but how am I going to get close enough to hear everything and still stay hidden?'

Just then all of the being came back with a large burst of whirl of air and flashing lights. In their arms one was carrying Adam and in another's arms was what I'm guessing to be Eve. They place Adam in the same position he was in when he had fallen asleep and gently laid Eve nearby.

"Awaken Adam," said the first being, "We have brought you a mate, one to help you and give you companionship like the other animals of this world," The being continued.

All of the talking woke Eve and she sat up quietly like a shy child with new company visiting.

"Eve, this is Adam your mate and companion. Your place is to help him keep the garden operational. Do you understand?" the being asked.

She nodded shyly. Adam walked over to her and gathered her hands into his with a smile.

"You are to help each other in all that you do. To take care of each other in all that happens. Do you both understand?" he asked looking at both of them. "I will return in a few days.

They both got busy taking care of the garden and the animals.

I'm not sure what happened. I don't remember sleeping but I do remember Adam and Eve making the clearing a little larger and playing together and laughing. Then there was that large gust of wind again and the being was back.

"Now that there has been changes made in your life, I have brought you a set of rules to live by. All of these rules are equal on all levels. These levels include mental, physical, emotional and spiritual others will be added as you grow in understanding. They are the same in the physical world, the same in mind, (that is what you think), the same in the emotional (that is what you feel) because all of these three sway the spiritual part of your being. Do you understand?" he asked looking at both Adam and Eve.

They both nodded. He started to explain these rules to them in detail. "You are not to kill. That means not in the physical, but it also covers emotional, mental or the spirit. There is no need to kill. You have all of the food you need and there is no animal here that will harm you. You are not to steal, not to take things that do not belong to you. That is meant physically taking something, so stealing another's idea, stealing another's joy, or stealing their life by wishing harm to them. You are not to lie to another soul or to yourself. Jealousy will do harm to yourself and can cause harm to others. If another has something you want, ask them for it or earn it. There will be others to join you as you grow. Cherish one another and care for each other with love and tenderness. And only eat what is supplied to you here in your garden. Do not eat anything that grows past your valley. Stay in your valley and all will be good with you." the being said.

They both nodded as if to say they understood and a great wind came and the being vanished.

"There is an innocence about these two that was so perfect. The animals could be understood and the plants were beautiful all of the animals get along. It is a perfect place to live." I reported.

Then one late afternoon Eve had finish all of her work and Adam had laid down for a nap. She decided to go for a short walk. They had both been told to stay in their valley and all would be well with them. But she had always wondered what was on the other side of the tall hill to the north of them. Just as she got to the top she noticed a tree that was a little different from the ones that were in their area. There were other strange things that she had never seen before. She was about to return to go tell Adam what she had found when she notice movement out of the corner of her eye. It shimmered as the sun hit it. She turned to face it and found a thin being in a shiny one piece suit holding out something toward her. She looked at him and noticed that his hand wasn't shinny like the rest of his body and stepped closer to take a better look. He touched her arm and she jumped back.

"Come let me show you things you have never dreamed of," he said softly with a smile.

Eve was very curious and wanted to learn all she could about everything. She and Adam had been told not to venture past certain boundaries and all would be well with them. But she felt the need to know and learn as much as she could about everything.

Just then he lean over touching her again with a kissed. She felt panic and she jumped away and ran back to where Adam was. He heard her come running into the clearing. Her mind racing she sat on one of the rocks and relived the touch she had felt. Adam wanted to know what had happened and she told him all and showed him what had happened.

I wonder to myself, 'if this is the tree that made the difference and took away the true harmony of life?'

"Where did this happen?" Adam asked.

"Come and I will show you." She said taking him by the hand.

As they got near the top of the hill the fruit on this tree almost started to glow very invitingly.

Eve reached out for one and as she did she could almost hear like a whisper in one ear. "Taste it. It's as good as it looks."

She took a bite and wanted more. She then offered it to Adam.

"Taste it. It is even sweeter than anything in our garden." She said holding the fruit out to him.

As he ate it she picked a few more to take back to the garden with them.

Just after they got back to the valley there was a large burst of air and the being that had brought him Eve was heard entering the clearing as he called for Adam. They hid, knowing that he could know their thoughts.

"Why are you hiding from me Adam come out and talk with me," he demanded.

"If he finds us, he may make me go away and not be with you. I want to stay with you." Eve whispered to Adam.

"Then we will stay hidden. If we are quiet then maybe he will go away." Adam said, hoping for the best. But in his heart he knew he had to come out of hiding.

When they came out they held branches with large leaves in front of themselves.

"Why are you holding the branches to hide yourselves from me?" he asked.

"We have no clothes," Adam said shyly.

"Who told you, you needed clothes?" he asked.

"Eve met a being on the high hill to the north and came telling and showed me what she had learned," he explained.

The being's face showed his unhappiness then seemed to be angered.

"We have given you everything you would ever need. You have known peace and tranquility. The animals all loved you and none of them would harm you or each other. You had fruits and vegetables to eat a good place to sleep and live. I gave you companionship and this is the way you repay me!" he said in a voice that was almost like thunder. "For your disobedience you will have to make it the best way you can. I will no longer allow you to stay in the garden. If you eat it will be the food you grow by your own hards work. Life will be harder than you have ever seen it. The animals will no longer be your friends just because you are alive." he added.

And with this the winds started to howled and as he left it started to rain. Adam and Eve ran to the larger tree for protection, but the water poured through the branches. They were frightened. They had never seen this happen before and the winds got colder and faster. They huddled in fear.

One of the other beings came back feeling a little sorry for them gave then animal skins to wear and then vanished almost as fast as he appeared.

Adam and Eve fashioned the skins so that their private parts were hidden from view and as they climbed the hill to the north, the garden started to die. Some of the animals growled at them as if to say "You caused this."

They made their way to the top of the hill and sat there all day watching the movement in the northern valley below. They weren't real sure what they were seeing, but they could see there was movement of some kind there.

The fruit of the tree that had looked, smelled and tasted so sweet just the day before now looked and smelled rotten and tasted awful. They felt confused but they sat there until late afternoon and hunger started to set in. They turned to start back to what they had once called home, but it wasn't there.

I had noticed while they sat and watched the movements in the valley below to the north that the area they had left sort of shifted, as if to dissolve.

After not seeing anything but an empty valley they decided to move a little closer in hopes of making out what it was that was moving in the valley below.

To their surprise there were other beings of some kind. Some of them were walking like man while others were

walking on all four legs or were just
hunched over. So they moved just a little
closer to see a little clearer.

As they sat behind a rock and tried
to keep a look out in all directions, Eve
noticed a tree about 30 steps away from
where they were sitting. It had fruit and
looked a lot like one they had taken care of
in the garden.

"Adam I think that tree may be like
one of the trees we took care of. It's not that
far away from us I want to go get some of
the fruit." Eve said.

"Keep your head low so whatever is
in the valley below doesn't see you." he
instructed.

"Okay," came the reply as she
started out almost crawling towards the
tree. But as she got closer she became a little
bolder and finally stood up when she got
closer to one of the lower limbs that held
out its fruit.

Just as she stood up a loud noise
came from the valley below. Beings on
what Adam had called horses came rushing
up from the valley floor. They surrounded
Eve.

Adam watched in amazement for a
short time. These beings were riding these
animals and they didn't seem to mind. At
that point he came out of hiding and

walked up to one of the horses and petted it on the cheek.

Adam's action took these two scaled green beings by surprise and they pointed something at him and Eve.

Adam and Eve had never seen anything like these beings or what they were holding.

The beings motioned for Adam and Eve to move toward the valley below. As they walked Eve handed Adam the fruit after taking a bite herself. It may have looked like one of the trees that had been in the garden but the fruit from it tasted almost bitter compared to the sweet ones they had been use to eating.

They were taken to a very large building covered in the shiny rocks they use to see in the garden streams. As the being shoved them with great force through the great shiny green doors and they almost fell to the floor. There were two great doors on both sides of them now and a grand almost empty room in front of them. But straight ahead of them they noticed a strange being that looked almost like them, except for his oversized ears that came to a point and an odd sized nose. He motioned for them to move closer with a pointed finger showing very long sharp nails.

"What were you doing near my favorite tree," came a very loud, almost earth shaking voice.

"We are new to your land and were getting hungry when we spotted the tree," Adam said with bowed head. 'He must be the one in charge here like God and the angels were in the garden.' he thought to himself.

"Where do you come from?" boomed the voice again. But this time Eve was sneaking a peek at the being when she heard it's voice.

She nudged Adam. "This being speaks without moving its mouth."

"Shhhhh, before you get us in trouble," he whispered.

Being the curious female she was, she couldn't hold back. "Excuse me your honor, we are new to your area and don't know your rules. We are sorry if we broke any of them. My name is Eve and this is Adam, we came from just beyond your tree," Eve said with a low bow.

Adam never raised his head. 'I dare not look up. I am afraid of what she has gotten us into now. She and the Guard Angles in the garden use to talk all of the time about different ways of doing things. She did manage to convince them to let her try experiments now and then. I do have to admit that some of them worked out pretty good. But here and how?' he thought to himself.

"Good what kind of work are you used to doing?" again boomed the ground shaking voice.

"We know the care of animals and plants. There were a lot of them from where we use to live."

"Good then you will be assigned to this kind of work here. Take them and show them what is required of them," the great voice demanded as the being closed its eyes and placed its hands in its lap.

"Two other beings came out of seemingly nowhere and grabbed them both by the arm and almost drug them through two other enormous doors to one side of the great room.

These two beings were even different from the ones they had already encountered. They had almost elephant looking heads. That is they had very large rounded ears and trunk like noses but shorter than the elephants they had known in the garden. These beings also walk upright but are very heavy footed, almost stomped with each step." I reported to Enah 2 (E 2).

They had watched the animals in the garden give birth, but here there seemed to be a lot of pain involved. "These animals seem to be in a lot of pain while giving birth." Adam whispered to Eve.

"Yes, I see that, I think that is what we were told before we left the garden. That life outside of the garden was going to be hard. I think this may be what we were told about." Eve replied.

But knowing that the animals were in pain bothered Adam and Eve. They had a hard time keeping up with the needs of all the animals being used by these beings.

Then came the day that Eve was to give birth to their first child and she remembered being told that there was going to be many changes in their lives because of her actions that ended their life in the garden.

Shortly after the birth they managed to sneak away and managed to get to the tree where they were first found. They looked in the direction of the garden and saw nothing but an empty barren valley where it once was.

Eve fell to the ground and cried. Adam knelt beside her and tried to console her. After a few minutes what she was told was brought back to her mind again but in clarity.

"Someday in the future God will supply a way for man to come back to the garden," she said looking up into Adams eyes. "One of the angels told me this before we left the garden. But life would be hard till then."

Everything started to fade from sight and I found myself back in the science lab with Enah 2 (E 2) standing nearby.

"So did all of that information get recorded," I asked, while looking around at the screen.

"Yes, we recorded it all and then remembered the writings did leave out a few small details and added a few like stories being passed on do sometimes, but the major parts were there.

I am glad that curiosity wasn't taken from life or we would all be stuck in a world of hurt. Not to say that sometime it can cause trouble too," Enah 2 (E 2) said laughing as I took off my helmet.

Chapter Eight
Meeting the Jinn

"Oh, hello Elaytay (Tay), Have you heard of a race called the Jinn?" Enah 2 (E 2) asked as I walked through the lab doors.

"No, can't say I have. What do we know about them?" I asked in return.

There was a pause in the conversation and I got to thinking about the party we were giving later in the evening for Kerzna (Kern) and his family.

Then I heard Enah 2 (E 2) saying, "Put on your helmet and get ready. We are starting the countdown. You are going to find out about the Jinn if you can find them."

I was a little confused 'if I can find them?'

"Okay." I put on my helmet and started to relax.

'This time I am surrounded by swirl of lights as I traveled to my destination. I guess there is a first time for everything.

But this felt odd. As they fade I find myself at the start of a new adventure. I think that is what I like most about doing this project.' I thought sort of chuckling to myself.

"I'm not sure what planet I am on, but it seemed to be a hot summer day because the sun seemed to be blazing extra warm. Even though I am walking on a shoreline, there's no breeze." That seemed very odd to me. "It looked a little like I could be on Earth but I'm not sure." I said hoping that Enah 2 (E 2) was able to hear me.

Enah 2 (E 2) didn't tell me where I was going this time. If he had, it didn't register. I remember him saying something about jinn.

My attention drifted to another time but was brought back quickly as a large bird sailed overhead with a loud screeching call. As I watched him fly off into the distance, my eyes fell back to the beach and that is when I spotted what looked to be a very pretty sea shell.

As I got closer to the shell I noticed a palm sized green bottle laying half buried in the sand nearby. I picked up the shell and placed it in my pocket and that is when I noticed that my hands were a different color and after looking a little closer, my clothes were different than what I would normally wear.

Just then the sun bounced off the bottle I had spotted earlier, drawing my attention back to it. I still wasn't sure where I was or what information I needed to gather. I tried listening for instructions from Enah 2 (E 2) but all I was getting was a soft static in my ear.

"I'm looking at the bottle lying in the sand I can see my reflection in it. I'm definitely dressed stranger than I'm used to. My pants are bloused like those in some of the old drawings I have seen in one of the museums, and it seemed that I'm wearing a turban on my head. I'm not dressed as a female and didn't look like myself. So I have to figure that this is a time in another place that I may have lived," I reported.

"I'm reaching for the bottle. OH! WOW!" I said with a start.

Enah 2 (E 2)'s voice was clear now, "What happened? We don't have visuals yet," he stated.

"When I touched the bottle there was a blue spark inside of it. It startled me and I almost dropped it. I'm holding it up between me and the blazing sun, but all I'm seeing is a light cloudiness inside. Other than that it seems completely empty," I reported.

"What else is close by? Is there a town or other people?" Enah 2 (E 2) asked.

"I'm not seeing anything else from where I'm standing. But there is a wall of sand leading away from the water," I said while looking around.

"Can you climb up to the top of the sand and see if there is anything else near you?" he asked.

"Sure," I answered quickly and started going up the sand dune.

My eyes just cleared the top of the dune when I spotted a village a short distance from my location.

"There seems to be a village a short distance from here. What do you want me to do? I don't know who or what I am at this point," I said just loud enough that Enah 2 (E 2) could hear me.

"Ok, first, put the bottle under your turban so no one will see it. You should be able to understand anyone who talks to you. Your translator is in place and turned on," he said.

No sooner had I put the bottle in place than I heard someone calling. I turned to see who it was.

"Someone has spotted me and is calling me Anobada (Noda). I'm not sure if that is my name or a greeting," I told Enah 2 (E 2).

"Tap your right ear to make sure you are translating right," he instructed.

The person called out louder, "Anobada (Noda), I thought we were to meet back at the mouth of the river."

"He seemed to be a little shorter than I am but dressed like I am. We both seem to be in our teens," I told Enah 2 (E 2) softly.

"Why are you looking at me so strangely?" he asked.

"Sorry I didn't know I was. I think I may have fallen and hit my head on something, because I don't remember anything." I explained.

"What are you talking about?" he asked looking around and back at me.

"It's like I just woke up and here I am. What is your name and why are we here?" I asked, looking straight at him.

"You must be kidding but ok. My name is Rahjina (Ray) and you are my older brother. We live with our mother just over the hill here. We come here to the beach each morning to look for special shells for mom. She makes jewelry to sell at the market. Now stop fooling around and tell me if you found any." He replied, seeming to be a little rushed.

"I only found this one." I said pulling it from my pocket and putting it in his hand.

"Have you seen any smooth stones yet?" he asked.

"No, were we to look for them too?" I questioned.

"Yes! Mom said shells, smooth stones and small pieces of drift wood." He answered quickly. "We have to be home before the sun reached the top of that tree, there." He said pointing at a tree near the shoreline down the beach a way.

"Okay," I said as I started to look around.

"You look closer to the shoreline and I will look inland," he instructed.

"Okay," I agreed.

I found a few more shells, some smooth stones and two small pieces of drift wood and placed them in a cloth bag I hadn't noticed earlier. It was like a belted purse tied to my waist, but hung from my right side.

Then I hear Rahjina (Ray) calling. "It's time for us to take what we found back to mom," as he came running towards me.

He motioned for me to follow him as he ran up the side of the sand dune. I managed to catch up with him and we walked into town together.

"Mom we are home. I think you will be happy with what we found this morning," he called out as we entered a dwelling that was made half of larger pieces of driftwood and tent as if from an old story I remembered reading a long time ago when I was younger.

"Put what you found on the work bench" she said while at the fire, working on cooking something.

"What are you making, mom?" Rahjina (Ray) asked. "Oh by the way Anobada (Noda) says he has lost his memory but doesn't seem to know how." Rahjina (Ray) added.

"Come here boy, let me look at you," she said motioning for me to come closer.

"Take a good look at her and let me see if I can placer," Enah 2 (E 2) said softly.

"I can see that she has coal black hair. I've seen these features before. I'm sure I will remember the place soon. Look at her clothing. I could only see a small amount at the edge of her multi colored scarf. She looks to be wearing a long brown cloth robe tied at the waist with a rope. The colored scarf is a sign that she is an artist of high ranking," Enah 2 (E 2) said.

She raised my eye lids and looked deeply into my eyes, as if to look deep into my being.

"You found something more than

just shells, stones and wood today. Didn't you?" she said softly as not to alert my brother.

I nodded slowly.

She let go of my head and looked closer at me. "Keep it to yourself. Let no one know. It can become dangerous for all of us. Do you understand?" She said looking at me sharply.

I nodded slightly again.

"We will talk more later," she added.

"Aw he will be ok. I think he just fell asleep in the sun and got over heated," she said loudly, pushing me away.

'I got the idea that the bottle was to remain a secret. I'm still not real sure what I found but I guess it's like a treasure.'

After our meal mom went over to inspect all of the things we had brought back from the beach.

"Anabahcla (Anna)! Are you home?" came a call from outside.

"Yes, you may enter," she called back as if she recognized the voice.

Then in the doorway stood a very tall slender man with a brilliant white turban adorned with a large ruby surrounded by bright blue sapphires.

Mom bowed low as he stepped farther into our house.

"I am pleased you came. I have my latest creations ready for you to see," she said while motioning him to draw closer to her work area.

After looking at a few of the things she had made, he said "Anabahcla (Anna), I think you have done a fine job on these. I am willing to pay you for these two pieces."

"Thank you I am honored," she said bowing low.

"And I will take these three as a gift," he said laying two coins on the table and sweeping up all of the jewelry on the table.

She bowed again "As you wish," she said.

He turned and left.

She went to the tent door and peeked through to make sure he was gone and then said. "That son of a dog! All he does is steal from all of us and dare any of us to make trouble. He knows that what he took today is worth five times what he gave me. He makes me so angry," she said almost gritting her teeth as she stamped the ground.

"What can we do about it mom?" I asked.

"Nothing," mom answered quickly. "And he knows it. He rules this whole area of the world and everyone is afraid of him

and the people he has working for him.
They follow his every rule without
thinking. It's like they have no brain."
Rahjina (Ray) said lowering his head.

"There is a caravan coming though
this area in about another ten days and I
think I have enough saved to join them. But
we will have to travel light. I have other
pieces of jewelry that I didn't show
tonight," she said putting her finger over
her lips to let us know to keep it a secret.
"Time for sleep, we have another day of
hunting tomorrow. Good night my sons."

"Good night mom" we said almost
at the same time.

I pulled off my turban very carefully
so Rahjina (Ray) didn't see the bottle.
Mom had hinted that there must be
something special about it when she looked
deeply at me earlier.

"Make sure that no one finds out
about the bottle." Enah 2 (E 2) said just as I
drifted off to sleep.

Morning came fast and when I
opened my eyes and looked around I could
see that Rahjina (Ray) was still asleep. I got
dressed quickly but made sure I didn't
make any noise.

Mom was already up and making
our first meal. She saw me and motioned
for me to come closer.

"Did you by chance find something special on the shore yesterday?" she whispered.

I nodded.

"Keep it very safe and don't let anyone know you have it. If it is what I think it is, it is worth more that you could ever think of," she whispered.

Just the Rahjina (Ray) came walking into the room.

Aw, Rahjina (Ray), good you're awake. Our meal is ready to eat. We have a long day ahead of us. Come sit down. I need to tell you both what is planned.

We all sat down and eat the small meal and gave thanks for what we had been given.

"Stay seated, we need to talk," mom said as she cleared the table.

She stacked the dishes for later and put away the small amount of food that was left then joined us at the table again.

"I know we don't have a lot of things but we need to pack up everything that is not going to be used in the next three days. And pack things as tight as you can. We will only have a small amount of room on the caravan for all that we have. It all has to be packed on one animal." She explained.

As we packed our belongings we

also had to decide if we really needed it or could it be replaced. We sorted and packed most of the day.

"Now we need to put all of the things we packed in the back dressing area of the tent so it is out of sight. No one is to know our plans. Do you both understand you are not to talk to anyone about our plans or our packing?" mom said in a low voice as if someone may be listening.

"Yes mom, we understand," we answered in unison.

"Now go find the things I need to make jewelry," she said pulling back the tapestry covering the door way.

I grabbed my shoulder bag and ran to catch up with Rahjina (Ray). It seemed normal for it to be a race as to see who could find the most items each time we went to gather things we think mom can use.

I managed to find a few perfect pieces of drift wood and a few shells that were just the right size right away. Rahjina (Ray) had gone down the shores in the other direction like he always did.

I decided to sit down just beyond a small sand hill out of eye sight from anyone walking alone the shore line. I wanted a better look at the bottle I had found.

I took off my turban and reached for

the bottle just as I heard Enah 2 (E 2)'s voice loud and clear as if the message was important. "Elaytay (Tay)! Whatever you do, <u>DO NOT</u> open the bottle." He said stressing the do not.

"Why?" I asked, waiting a little before picking up the bottle.

"The bottle you found looks a lot like the old drawings of the kinds of bottles used to hold the Jinn." He explained.

"Jinn?" I questioned. "Do you mean the people that can appear out of smoke? I remember now hearing a little about them when I was very young." I added.

"Yes and like most people some are nice and some aren't so nice." He replied.

"But I have always wanted to meet one, and no one else is around, so I don't see any harm" I replied.

"You must promise to listen and do as I tell you after you open the bottle. DO YOU PROMISE?" he said almost demanding an answer.

"Yes, I will listen for your voice." I answered reluctantly.

I proceeded to twist and pull on the stopper slowly as not to damage the bottle.

Just as I eased the stopper the last little bit a slow stream or what looked like steam or white smoke came from the bottle. As it rose into the air I could make out what looked to be a human like form.

Then a voice of what sounded friendly said. "Greetings young master. I am Bazalar (Baz), your humble servant. What is it that you wish of me?" he asked.

"Ask if he is a Jinn that grants wished and if so how many?" Enah 2 (E 2) said almost too loud.

Bazalar (Baz) must have heard Enah 2 (E 2) because he questioned. "Do you need this information or want it for your friend?"

"For both of us if you don't mind, please." I said.

"Well then your answer is; it all depends upon what kind of things you wish for." Bazalar (Baz) said, resting his hands on his hips.

"Can anyone else see you?" I asked.

"Not if you don't want them too," he informed me.

"I think it would be safer for both of us if others couldn't see you." I said quietly.

"Then it is done," Bazalar (Baz) said with the tinkling of a bell.

"Good, can I ask you questions?" I want to know more about you and where you come from." I asked.

"Of course, you are the master. What do you have need to know?" he asked folding his arms and sitting on the sand in front of me as if we were great friends.

"Thanks. How did you get in the bottle?" I asked listening closely for the answer.

"That may be a little hard to explain. But on my home planet we have a lot of rules to live by and sometimes when we are young it is hard to follow all of them to the letter of the law. When someone disobeys one of the laws, no matter how small, our punishment is to spend time in confinement. We are confined to inter-dimensional space and the physical form can show up as a bottle, lamp, stone or some other article and then we are deposited on other planets until our time is served," he explained while looking at the ground as if he was ashamed.

"So what did you?" I asked.

"There was a girl in my village I liked a lot and I slipped out one night on a full moon to sit in the garden with her, I was caught coming home. It was past the time we were allowed out of our homes." He explained.

"Wow that sound like a big punishment for such a small thing." I replied. "That bottle seems really small." I added.

"Well size isn't the problem because

the inside is in a different dimension that has a different space and time frame that yours does," Bazalar (Baz) explained almost smiling. "It's the being alone that is hard. The only time I can be out of the bottle is when I am working for others." He added.

"So how do they know when you are not helping someone? I mean right now we are just talking." I questioned.

"Yes, but I am helping you by answering your questions. But after I have answered your questions or done completing your need then I am automatically summoned back into my bottle." Bazalar (Baz) explained.

"What happens if your bottle gets broken?" I asked.

"Whatever we are placed in reassembles itself as it was before it was destroyed." He explained.

"So how do you know when your time is up and you are free?" I asked.

"Well because time for us is a lot different from on other planets, we can out live many, many, generations. The time we have to serve depends on what we did in order to get put away." He said trying to explain.

"So how do you know when you are free?" I asked again.

"I guess I will know when I have finished helping someone and I don't get swept back into the bottle." He said with a slight smile.

"Do you know how long you have been in the bottle already?" I asked.

"Not really. Because for me there is no time in the bottle, it is always the present." He explained.

"I've heard that some Jinn only give the person finding them a limited amount of wishes. Are you told to only give each person a certain number of wishes or only help them so much?" I asked.

"I wasn't told only to give a limited amount to each person. But helping others is the only way we can get out of the bottle. So it sort of depends if we really want to help a certain person. Some people don't make it easy to like them or want to help them and some that I have met got greedy a short time after I met them, or their attitude changes and you really don't want to be around them." He explained.

"Are there certain wishes I would be expected to make?" I asked.

"Financial wealth is the normal wish, or materialistic things that they could get on their own if they worked really hard at a great paying job. Some ask for things like large fancy houses/palaces or out laddish transportation. But we do have our limits as to what we can do." He informed me.

"Like what kinds of limits?" I asked.

"Well, we can't heal illnesses or bring the dead back to life. We can't make a being younger or improve their health. Those kinds of things are only in the Creator's hand. But we are allowed to impersonate a loved one or a person of importance to another in order to help relieve stress or trapped emotions. But we are not allowed to interact with anyone at that time. We are only allowed to smile or nod from across a short distance. We are also not allowed to do damage to another living being without adding more punishment to our own lives. We are allowed to help each individual being as much or as little as we want to." He explained.

Enah 2 (E 2) whispered a few more questions into my ear, letting me know what kind of information they were wanting.

"I was told once that Jinn only had so many wishes to fill and then they would be free. Is that true?" I asked.

"No, we are expected to help as needed and we do have to grant at lease a certain number of wishes, but granting that number of wished is not an automatic release. We can grant to each master according to what we want as long as we want. We hold the right to withhold any number of wishes over three if we think the master is unworthy of any more help." He explained.

"So what kinds of acts would make a person unworthy of your extra help?" I asked.

"If a master was unkind, greedy, mean to others, or spiteful, things like that. In cases like that we can ask to be place somewhere else and the item we are trapped in can vanish and be places somewhere else." He said with a smile. "Is there anything you wish me to help you with right now?" he asked.

"I can't think of anything I need at this time. But thank you for the visit and information." I said with a nod.

"Then I ask to be relieved at this time young master," he requested.

"Okay," I agreed.

Within seconds he was back in his bottle and I had just put the bottle away and my turban on when I hear Rahjina (Ray) calling for me.

"Anobada (Noda)! Where are you? We have been gone for hours and mom will be worried." He yelled.

"I'm here," I said standing up and dusting the sand off my pants.

"What are you doing there? We were to be hunting for things mom can use." He said, sounding a little irritated.

"I was looking at the things I had found and sort of day dreaming about them." I said hoping he hadn't heard me talking to Bazalar (Baz).

"Well come on we need to get home." He said as he took off running.

I had to run faster to catch up with him.

"Oh good you got back just in time to eat. Put the things you found today on the work table and wash up quickly." Mom said almost laughing.

While drying my hands I asked. "Did something happen to make you extra happy today?"

"Yes, I got word today that the caravan will be passing through here in two days and they have an extra pack animal for us," she announced.

"Good, but I was wondering how are we going to slip out without getting caught," I asked.

"I'm not real sure yet. I haven't planned that far ahead." She said seeming to give it deep thought.

"I have friends that live at the outer

edge of town. Maybe we can store our things there till we leave," Rahjina (Ray) suggested.

"I'm not sure who all we can really trust at this point." Mom said hesitating to think about it. "That would be a lot to ask of anyone," she added.

"We will figure out some way that will be safe for all of us," I said looking up from my plate at mom.

"I'm sure we will," she said giving me a wink, "You haven't said anything to anyone about us moving have you Rahjina (Ray)?" she said looking deeply straight at him.

"Nno-o-o mom," he said almost shuttering.

"Ok, what did you say and to whom?" she said sternly.

Somehow mom seemed to be able to look through us. She knew things before they happened and could read us like an open book. But Rahjina (Ray) still tried getting past her with things.

"W e l l .., I may have hinted about moving to my friend at the edge of town," Rahjan said slowly.

"I can't believe you would do that. You know the way things are and how much danger we can be in if the wrong persons finds out. Didn't I make it clear enough that it was to be a secret?" mom said sternly, looking straight at Rahjina (Ray).

"Yes mam, but he is my best friend and I'm sure he wouldn't say anything. I thought maybe we could put some of our things at their place." he said looking at his feet. "Sorry." he added.

"We can manage just find. I'm sure it will work out. DO NOT mention anything to anyone else in any form. Do you understand!" mom said strongly to get her point through to both of us.

We both nodded in unison.

"Okay enough about this. Bow your heads and let's give thanks for our meal." She said looking at both of us.

"This is really good mom." I said with a smile, hoping to change the energy in the room.

"Thank you. After we eat and finish cleaning up, I need you two to carry these things to the back area." She said pointing to a pile of packed bundles stacked in one corner. "I packed those while you two were at the beach." She added.

Time seemed to fly by and it was time to sleep, but my mind was racing so fast it was hard to keep my eyes closed. I had become so completely occupied with this life's adventure I hadn't noticed that I hadn't heard anything from Enah 2 (E 2).

We were to meet up with the caravan tomorrow after dark. I guess I was a little worried about how that was going to work out. The leader of this village refused to allow any of his craftsmen to leave. Especially craftsmen like my mom who made special one of a kind jewelry pieces for his wives and his powerful friends. It was as if he owned all of the families in our area.

It seemed that I had just fallen asleep when mom was stroking my arm and saying it was time to get up. It wasn't quite daylight yet.

Mom woke us both. "I think we should start getting things moved now." she said softly. "We need to keep quiet so as not to alert anyone else in camp." She added holding her finger up to her lips. "Get dressed quickly but quietly." She said walking toward the back of our living quarters.

We got dressed and followed her. She was stacking the bundles she wanted moved first.

"I want the two of you to carry all of these to the last watering hole east of here. Place them behind the small trees there and Rahjina (Ray), I want you to stay there and keep watch over our things. Anobada

(Noda) I need you to be the runner between. You will be taking our things to were Rahjina (Ray) will be waiting for you." she whispers looking at both of us. "Rahjina (Ray), you are to stay with all of our things till I can get there. You are not to leave them for any reason. DO YOU UNDERSTAND ME?" she questioned looking deeply into Rahjina (Ray)'s eyes.

"Yes mam. I am to stay put no matter what happens." He said in a low voice.

"Good, help your brother on this trip and then stay put." She said just to make sure there was no misunderstanding. "Make sure no one sees you." She instructed.

We gathered up all of the bundles we could carry and headed for the area mom had sent us to. We had to move fast but very quietly as not to waken anyone along the way. The watering hole mom was sending us to was a little over an hour away and if we were to run, someone may hear the sound of fast feet. It is hard to run with such heavy bundles without making a sound, so we moved slowly but quietly from shadow to shadow. We knew we could move a little faster once we got past the tribal peoples who lived near the path we had to take.

I helped Rahjina (Ray) stack the bundle so they couldn't be seen and made sure he knew to stay out of sight and then assured him I would be back with more as soon as I could.

I had to make sure we had all of the bundles moved before the sun started to break over the dunes, so I cut across country to make it back to mom a little faster than walking the normal path. I had to take the path with the bundles because it was a cleared path.

"Good here is the next load to be taken." Mom whispered as I walked through the door. "Did you find the place I was talking about?" She asked while I was tying and stacking the bundles for easier carrying.

"Yes mom and I made sure to tell Rahjina (Ray) to stay out of sight before I left him." I said grabbing the last bundle.

"Good, hurry now before the first light." She whispered with a pat on my shoulder.

I hurried as fast as I could to where Rahjina (Ray) and I had stacked the first load of bundles.

I didn't see Rahjina (Ray) anywhere. This was disturbing to me but I didn't have time to wait or to hunt for him if I was to get everything mom had packed to this spot. I place the load I had behind some other brush nearby. My thought was that if Rahjina (Ray) had gotten caught I didn't want who ever had him to find out that I had made another trip. I could only keep my figures crossed as is said and hope that he hadn't talked to anyone in the area about our plans.

I ran as fast as I could back to where mom was and still remain quiet.

"What is happening?" she asked as soon as I got to the door. Mom always seemed to know when something wasn't right. I explained what had happened and she helped to gather the last of the bundles. She had packed a few other things while I was gone. "Okay then this will have to be the last of our things then. We can take no chances of getting caught." She said gathering up the last three bundles. "We have to move quickly and quietly to our meeting spot." She added as we walked out of the door and she closed the enter door very quietly.

We made it to the meeting point without making a sound and we placed the bundles with the others I had left the last time.

"Mom, did you say that the caravan wasn't to be here till tonight?" I whispered.

"Yes but I got word that they were

coming early and were going to try and sort of sneak by so they didn't have to deal with Ahragaja (Rag). They didn't want to pay his prices for the food and water he had in town waiting for them." She said.

"I left Rahjina (Ray) right over there with the bundles we brought out the first time. But when I came back he wasn't there so I left the second load here. I wanted to make sure that everything was ok before putting everything we owned in one place." I explained.

"Good thinking, but we need to do a little searching to find out where he is." She said while looking through the brush toward the water hole. "I see movement near the water." She said pointing to the eastern most point.

"I will go that way to see if I can spot him," I said picking up our water jug.

As I got closer I could see Rahjina (Ray) talking to someone but couldn't make out who it was. I went closer to fill the water jug but I didn't want the person he was talking to know Rahjina (Ray) was my brother until I knew the situation.

"Greetings.' I said as I walked up. "How is the water this morning?" I asked watching the response.

"Anobada (Noda), my brother." Rahjina (Ray) said looking at the person he had been talking to. "Where are the rest of mom's bundles?" he asked.

"They are safe where ever they are. Who is this?" I asked while studying his reactions.

"This is the leader of the caravan, Galzenadar(Glen)." Rahjina (Ray) said with his hand opened toward Galzenadar(Glen).

"Where is the caravan? I asked.

"Oh not to worry they are near." He answered slowly.

"Good I heard that the caravan wasn't getting into town till tomorrow night." I said.

"There was a change because of a few things we heard along the way." He said looking around.

"If you get a chance take a look at the back of his left hand." Enah 2 (E 2) said softly in my ear. "You are looking for a small spider web above the webbing of his thumb." He added. "If he is the real leader the web will be there. There is also two red dots over his right eye. You may have to ask him to raise his head cover." Enah 2 (E 2) suggested.

"Can you take off your head cover? I would like to see who I am talking to." I asked.

"Oh, truly not a problem, I forgot I

had it on. After all it is starting to get lighter out here." He said reaching for his covering with his left hand.

I could see the web and then I spotted the red dots. Take me to your caravan. I would like to see it." I said

"Good thinking the body marking can always be faked." Enah 2 (E 2) whispered.

He started to walk towards the east. Rahjina (Ray) started to follow him. I caught Rahjina (Ray) by the arm. "What all have you told this man?" I asked quietly.

"I spotted him getting water and figured he was the person we were waiting for. I asked if he was the caravan leader and he said yes. I told him we were the one that were to meet him here." Rahjina (Ray) said.

"You better pray he is, because if he isn't then we are all in danger." I said soft enough that Galzenadar(Glen) couldn't hear.

"They are on the other side of this dune." He almost shouted as he started to climb the sand dune.

Somehow all of this just didn't feel quite right. I looked back over my shoulder and I could see mom holding up the edge of her head wrap with her hand over her mouth. Then she went back into the higher bushes. I could tell by her actions that she didn't think we were safe.

I reached out and grabbed Rahjina (Ray)'s arm. We had just started a few feet up the dune. "Stop, there is danger." I said just loud enough for him to hear.

"Galzenadar(Glen), We will catch up with you, we are going to get our bundles." I shouted with a wave. And I almost had to drag Rahjina (Ray) back down the dune.

When I looked back toward Galzenadar(Glen), he was just disappearing over the dune. We walked back to the water hole and mom caught up with us.

"That was not the caravan leader." she said.

"How do you know mom?" I asked.

"Because the leader of the caravan we were to meets wears a dark green and white head dress, not a black one." She said watching the dune. "And the caravan would be coming from that direction." She added pointing more to the south. They will be bringing in the camels and water barrels to get filled. They won't be hiding behind a dune. We need to hide until we see them." she explained. "Rahjina (Ray) what did you do with the things that were left with you?" she asked.

"I left then in the bushes over there." He pointed to a bush a few feet from the ones I had left him in. "I got thirsty and went for a drink. That is when Galzenadar(Glen) came walking up from that direction." He explained pointing towards the dune he had just gone over.

"Okay, then we will just sit right here until we see the right group come in for water. They wouldn't be traveling by night. So I am thinking they should be here in a few hours." She said and we all sat down and got comfortable.

Time seemed to go very slow but finally a camel's head came bobbing just above the dune to the south east. "Wait !" mom said. "We will be patient and see what happens. Our bundles are to go in the large bags of a camel with a red head harness." She explained.

So we sat in the underbrush and watched. "We are to sneak the bundles into the bags without attracting attention. I know that may seem hard but this one will be made to kneel to drink water." She added.

"I think I see the one you are talking about. He just came over the dune. Is that the one mom?" I asked.

"It looks like the one that was described. But let's wait a little long to see what part of the water pool he is taken to." She whispered. "I hope it will be near the brush closest to us." She added.

"Shouldn't we start moving our bundles a little closer so we are ready when his trainer makes him kneel?" I asked.

"Yes. But we should do it slow and try to stay below the brush level so no one will see us." Mom instructed. "I will put the first bundle in so that the trainer knows that I am the one that made the deal, and I need to let him know about Galzenadar(Glen)." She said quietly.

We carried only a few bundles at a time so we could stay below the height of the lowest brush.

"Is this the last bundle?" mom whispered looking at me.

"Yes, this is the last of them." I said peeking through an opening in the leaves.

"I will go talk the trainer of the marked camel and make sure it is the right one. When we walk to the other side of the camel, I need you to start loading the bundles." Mom instructed.

I nodded and she started to walk toward the trainer with one of the bundles in hand. It wasn't long before they walked to the other side of the camel and talked for a long time. Rahjina (Ray) and I loaded the bundles as quickly as we could.

There were only two left to pack. As I went toward the brush to gather them Rahjina (Ray) ran toward the dune that

Galzenadar(Glen) had walked over.

I grabbed the last two bundles and hurried towards mom and explained what Rahjina (Ray) was doing.

I could see Rahjina (Ray) running up the dune and he was nearing the top as the trainer made the camel stand. This gave the others a sign that it was time to leave.

All of the other trainers gathered the camels and started toward the dune they had come over. The trainer mom had been talking to helped her to climb up and sit in the seating that had been in place on the camel all this time. I hadn't really noticed it. I ran alongside with the trainer.

Mom started to cry. She didn't want to leave Rahjina (Ray) behind but there wasn't really anything she could do about it. There was a good chance that Galzenadar(Glen) was working for the main chief of the community we were being held by.

"Mom, I promise I will come back for him when I know you are safe." I promised. "After all I know I can do this. I will bring him later if he wants to come." I added, both of us knowing that you can't force a person to be what you want them to be, if they don't want to.

"Thank you. You are a good son. I know you will do the right thing when the time is right." She said.

Just then the trained smacked the camel on the side and it started moving faster. I had to run to keep up.

One of the people on the caravan tossed me an over drape to help me blend in with the rest of the group, and my turban was already a common color so that helped.

We traveled as fast as we could but we could see that Galzenadar(Glen) group was catching up with us. They were only about a hour from us now.

I looked up at mom and pulled off my turban. She seen the bottle and nodded.

I made a passing rub and pulled out the stopper of Bazalar (Baz)'s bottle. He showed himself only to me. I explained the situation to him.

"What do you wish me to do young master?" he asked.

"Can you place Galzenadar(Glen) and his group somewhere else in the desert at least five days from us even at his fastest speed. Maybe make them a little lost for a while. We need to get away and be safe. I don't want them hurt. We just need time to get away free." I explained.

Bazalar (Baz) gave a small laugh and agreed. With the way of his hand, they were nowhere in sight. "It is done young master. It will take them many days to catch you if they can figure out where they are." And he laughed even deeper. "That was fun. Thank you." He said.

I held up the bottle and he bowed and went back in.

Just then I hear Enah 2 (E 2), "Well done. Now it is time for you to come back to us." He said with a chuckle.

The next thing I knew I was opening my eyes, sitting in my chair in the control lab.

"What an adventure." I said as I took off my helmet and got up from my chair. "Wow, what a rush." I said laughing. "Is that the last one for this sestron (today)?" I added.

"Yes, we will see you in the morning." Enah 2 (E 2) said as he finished checking the equipment and making notes.

Chapter Nine
The Canyons of Venus

"Good amacron (morning) Elaytay
(Tay), Are you ready for another adventure?"
Enah 2 (E 2)'s voice busted through the
silence as I walked through the lab doors. I
had been lost in thoughts of a planned
camping trip in the mountains of Obiskis this
weekend.

"Doing great and yes, ready to go." I
said as I sat down in my chair.

Just then one of the control operations
persons came to let us know there was a
short hold on the mission because of a
technical issue.

"I'm ready when everything is set." I
said holding my helmet in my lap.

"Sir, we will be ready in about ten
keptrons (minutes)." a voice from the other
side of the room came through Enah 2 (E 2)'s
communication console.

So I put on my helmet, sat back and

started the relaxing part of my mission. That was the first part of every mission, to sit quietly, slow my breathing and relax every muscle.

"Okay, Ready for count down." Enah 2 (E 2) said.

I gave thumbs up and I was off swirling through what looked a little like thin clouds.

"Wow what a night," I said as I woke up.

I must not have slept well. I stood up and looked around. "It seems I'm in a young person's bedroom and the room seems to be round. I found a mirror." I said under my breath so Enah 2 (E 2) would know what was happening. "Wow, I look a little stranger than I'm use to looking at. I have yellow eyes and my skin has a light orange tint and my hair is a soft brown." I continued. I wasn't sure if Enah 2 (E 2) had visuals yet.

"I found a picture of me with what I figure is family. Everyone's skin is a little different. Some are darker or lighter than mine. I kind of think I must me in my mid-teens. But I don't seem to remember much about my life," I added.

"ZANEWNA (ZANE)!, morning meal is ready. Hurry you only have a short time before the glider will be here." said a voice beyond the bedroom door.

"Okay, coming." I replied as I walked towards the bedroom door. I opened it slowly not sure of what I would find on the other side.

"I'm still not remembering anything about this life Enah 2 (E 2)." I said quietly.

"Hello?" I called out as I opened the door and stepped through the doorway.

As I did this very strange looking animal came bounding around the corner of the long hall that lay out in front of me,

"Whatever it is, it seems to be friendly. It likes to lick me, I just hope it's not tasting me." I said almost laughing. "It tickles." I added.

"Describe this animal to me. Our visuals are still a little distorted." Enah 2 (E 2) said.

"Well, its fur is light blue with green and black spots, it has long ears, and very large eyes with the whites showing all the way around the bright green pupils. It has 2 antenna coming from its' head and strange ridges across its nose and forehead. Oh, and it has six legs, a curled bushy tail and a very long tongue." I said softly while petting it. I think it maybe what we would consider from the canine group.

Just then I hear the voice calling again. "Zanewna (Zane) hurry!" I think that must be my name.

"Coming." I answered quickly.

As I rounded the corner I could smell something good but wasn't sure what it was. It seemed familiar but I couldn't place it.

"Sit down and eat the glider will be here soon." Came the voice again from behind a short divider wall of the large room I was about to enter from the long hall.

"I'm not sure what is happening here. I'm seeing myself in the mirror earlier, but that is all I know. I don't remember this life." I whispered to inform Enah 2 (E 2) before walking into the main room.

As I looked around I spotted the woman in the photo I had seen earlier. 'That must be my mom.' I thought.

"Zanewna (Zane), sit down and eat." She said as she turned around to face me. I see you're dressed, but your hair is a mess and you have on the wrong shoes. And where is your helmet?" she asked

I guess I looked a little confused.

"Are you okay?" she asked.

"I have a sore spot on my head. Are you my mom?" I asked.

"No hun, I'm you Aunt Marzla (Aunt Mars) (Aunt Mars), you mom's sister." She answered.

"Where is my mom?" I asked.

"We lost both of them on their last mission a little over a year ago." She said

"What do you remember about yesterday?" she asked.

"Nothing, I don't remember anything. I didn't know my name till you called me earlier." I said still confused and completely blank about where I was or what was going on.

"I think maybe you should stay home today. Maybe you will remember more as the day goes by." She said.

"What do I do at work? Where do I work?" I quizzed.

"You're a scientist and are experimenting with insulation for shielding our ships and homes from the heat." She explained "Don't you remember any of that?" she asked.

I went and looked out of the window before sitting down to eat. "Why is our sky orange?" I asked.

"It's been that way for eons." She said looking strangely at me. "What other color would it be?" she questioned tilting her head to one side.

"I don't know it just seems odd." I said, wondering just what planet I was on. I wasn't really given any information as to where I was going or what I was to find out this time. Or if I was given the information it didn't register.

"Sorry we just don't have much

information on the history of Venus." Enah 2 (E 2) said softly.

"I think I must have hit my head on something yesterday." I said.

"Why do you say that?" Aunt Marzla (Aunt Mars) asked.

"I have a sore spot right there." I said pointing to a spot on the right side of my head.

"Wow, you have quite a lump there." She said gently feeling my head. Maybe we should take you for a checkup today and make sure you didn't do any damage. Do you remember how it happened?" she added.

"No, I don't remember anything from before I woke up this morning." I said. "I just know it hurts to touch it." I added pulling her hand from my head.

"Oh, Sorry dear. You finish your meal and I will make arrangement to get you checked." She said going to a display screen which showed up when she patted the air in front of her. It hung in midair and was visible from both sides.

Soon a man came on asking what she needed. "It seems that my niece woke this morning with a lump on her head and can't remember anything prior to waking this morning." She told him.

"Bring her in. We can run the scans within the hour." He said and then vanished.

There was nothing left of the screen that had been hanging in midair moments before. "That was strange." I said.

"What?" she questioned.

"Being able to talk to a person in midair like that." I explained.

"That technology has been around for a very long time. That must have been a very hard bump you got. Do you remember anything about what you were doing yesterday?" she asked while putting on her jacket. "Go get your jacket." She added.

I went back to my bedroom and looked around for a jacket. All I found was a very light weight blue jacket. It didn't look like it would keep one warm. It was even thinner that my wind jacket I had at home. I put it on and joined my Aunt Marzla (Aunt Mars) at the front door.

"Pull your hood up." She instructed. "The heat is bad out this time of day." She added. "Luckily we don't have far to go. We only lived a short distant to the medical facility." She added.

As we stepped outside I could get a better view of the area we lived in. The only plants I saw were growing under coverings. I could see that the light was able to go through them but it looked like the taller plants had been trims so they could stay under the covering.

I had to ask. "Why is it that the only vegetation is growing under the coverings?"

"Our heat shields are starting to fail. The heat above the canyons have gotten hotter through the eons and the shields are getting old now and need to be replaced. That is what you have been working on for the last few years. You said you were getting closer. You were able to hold higher heat at bay with what you had so far but you wanted to push it to an even stronger shield. We are using a double shield with space between for our entry and exit points for our ships now." She explained.

It was then that I noticed the canyon walls on either side. It reminded me of the great canyon I remember seeing on Earth when I was there. This canyon was so wide that there was a large city in the middle with plenty of room to expand. It didn't seem that air and water was a problem. So I was now wondering 'why is it so hot?'

"What is making the sky orange?" I asked

"The fire." Aunt Marzla (Aunt Mars) said looking at me very strangely. "What do you remember about your life and this planet?" she asked.

"Nothing before I woke up this morning." I replied again.

"The Fire?" I probed. I needed to

know more.

"Yes, well we can get into that a little later. We are here now, let's take care of you and see why you can't remember anything earlier than is morning. Sit down over there." Aunt Marzla (Aunt Mars) insisted pointing to a corner where I spotted a few lonely chairs and a few picture books. The picture told a story of their own, but there was a strange batch of characters under each one. I didn't recognize any of the characters. I looked over a few other books and papers that were on the table in front of me. But it was the same story each time. I had no idea what they were talking about. I figured they were in a different language than I was used to reading.

My aunt came over and sat down beside me. "Did you find something to read?" she asked.

"Some of them look interesting but they all seem to be in a different language." I explained.

"Let me see." She said taking the one I was looking at. "No they are in our language. Are you saying you can't read them?" she queried.

"I have no clue what they are saying other than looking at the pictures." I said being even more confused than I already was.

"Oh my, you must have hit your head harder than I thought. It's a good thing our doctors can scan for problems. Maybe they can find out what is causing your memory loss and fix it." She said looking worried.

"I hope so it would be nice to know what all I knew before I got the lump on my head." I said with a slight smile.

The doctor's assistant came through the double doors and announced it was time for me to be checked.

"Okay hun, let's get this done and see what can be done to bring back your memory." Aunt Marzla (Aunt Mars) said motioning towards the doors being held open by the assistant.

We walked into a room with a large comfortable looking chair and around it were panels of instruments and a lot of wires with a helmet hooked to some of them.

"I'm not sure what to expect and feel a little hesitant." I whispered under my breath just loud enough for Enah 2 (E 2) to hear.

"It's okay it won't harm you here. Let them do the tests." He urged.

"Don't be afraid. I will explain everything I'm going to do before I do anything. Okay?" the tech explained. "By the way my name is Esentia (Sent)." She said smiling.

She seemed pleasant enough. She had

bright orange hair with darker streaks running through it and it was pulled to the back of her head in a small bun. Her skin was almost yellow and she had large emerald green eyes. She was a slim person and just a little taller than me.

I looked over at my Aunt Marzla (Aunt Mars) and she gave me a nod as to say it's okay.

Esentia (Sent) motioned for me to take a seat in the big chair. I walked over and sat down slowly.

"Make yourself comfortable, these test can take a while." Esentia (Sent) said with a smile.

After I got settled, Esentia (Sent) brought the helmet and put it in my lap. "Take a look at it if you want. I am going to put it on your head and then this rotating arm will rotate around you and take some reading. This is to make sure you didn't do any physical harm to the outside of your head." She explained.

To this I said "Okay." And put it on.

"Sit real still or we will have to do it again." She instructed.

After she pushed a few buttons and flipped a switch or two there was a high pitched squeal. I couldn't help but say "yaweee" out loud while putting my hands over my ears, which didn't help.

"Are you hearing a high pitch sound?" Esentia (Sent) questioned while standing directly in front of me.

"Yeeessss! Make it stop." I said feeling like I was yelling.

Esentia (Sent) went and flipped another switch and it stopped. But them there was a low pitch hum and almost caused my jaw to lock.

"Ummmm!" I said motioning to my jaw. It felt as if it was being restrained from some outside force and was locked in place.

"Oh sorry, but I need to finish with all of the tests to see all of the damages." Esentia (Sent) said sympathetically.

My aunt looked on giving me a grimacing smile as if to say she wished it wasn't so painful but it had to be done to find a cure and get my memory back.

After about twenty minutes of many painful sounds Esentia (Sent) said "All done with that test."

My head still pounding from the all the vibration it had just been through but I managed to ask. "Through with this test? You mean there are more?" I asked.

"Oh yes. That one was to see if you had cracked to the outer layers of your skull and if so how deep. The next ones are for your brain. We need to find the damaged area and get it fixed. You did say you didn't know anything when you woke up this morning? Right?" she said informing me and making sure she had the facts right.

"Yes." I said slowly.

"Well the sound vibrations let me know where the damage was and how deep it went on your skull. Now we need to find out what part of your brain was damaged the most." She explained.

"It will all be ok." Aunt Marzla (Aunt Mars) said patting me on the shoulder for reassurance as we walked down a long hall that was painted leaf green with a long orange stripe running the length of the hall about shoulder height. As we walked I could hear each of our footsteps on the dark marble floor. It was almost hypnotic like a musical beat.

"This is our next stop." Esentia (Sent) said opening a large blue door.

As she opened the door the smell of lilacs waffled through the air. Then I wonder how I remembered the name of that flower or even knew it was a flower.

"I like the smell of lilacs." I said.

"Of What?" Aunt Marzla (Aunt Mars) asked. "Li lacs?" she questioned.

"It's a flower." I replied still puzzles as to why I knew that name from somewhere.

"I've never heard of it. Where is it found?" Esentia (Sent) queried wanting more information.

"I'm not sure. When I caught the smell the name popped into my head. That's all I know." I said shrugging my shoulders.

"It's not in our data bases." Esentia (Sent) said tapping her wrist band.

I had been looking at the floor. The spots where I was standing was slowly changing colors. Then I noticed it was only changing under people's feet. It wasn't changing under anything else in the room. I looked around at the rest of the room and there seemed to be a lot of blinking panels with switches, knobs and levers on the walls.

"Don't be scared." My aunt said patting me on the back.

I guess she could see I was a little scared and confused.

There was a long exam table in the middle of the room with a few machines with long robotic arms standing close by. Then I spotted trays of surgical tools standing next to each of the machines.

Just seeing them made me feel real uneasy. My imagination raced like the fastest spaceship ever made. I had no idea what to expect and I felt like running but my feet felt as if they were stuck to the floor.

Esentia (Sent) noticed my uneasiness and said. "Don't worry. Sit over here and smell this flower for a few minutes."

As I sat down she handed me a beautiful flower. I sat there and looked at it for a while. It seemed to change colors but more slowly than the floor. It started with a lite sky blue with a white base like clouds drifting on a clear day on Earth. Then it started changing to the peaceful purples with swirls of lite pink like the clouds in the skies of Cyterrious.

"Go ahead and take a few beep breaths while you smell it. This flower smells real nice." Esentia (Sent) said with a smile.

So I took a long deep breath and took in the most pleasing smell from this flower. The next thing I knew, I was floating above my body.

"Enah 2 (E 2) this is very strange. Can you hear me? I can't move and I seem to be floating but Zanewna (Zane)'s body is being moved to the exam table." I said or thought as strongly as I could.

"We can only sense that there is movement of the body but we can't see anything right now. We have to shift communications to observer mode." Enah 2 (E 2)" voice came though as a thought in the center of my head which was a little strange. I had gotten used to hearing his voice in my ear.

This is the first time we had to communicate in observer mode. "Yes, we have visual now. And you do seem to be floating above the host's body." He confirmed. "Were you told what they were going to do?" he asked.

"No, I have no idea. I guess we will watch and see." I said floating a little closer so I could see all that was happening.

Zanewna (Zane)'s body was lying on the table propped on her right side so she couldn't move. Her head was in a device that looked like a clamp and her hands and legs were strapped to the table so she couldn't move them.

A young male about Zanewna (Zane)'s age in a long pale yellow smock came to the table and took some of the instruments from each of the surgical trays and fit them into the robotic arms. Then a female is a violet smock trimmed in a darker purple came and started typing putting information into the machines. The machines with arms started moving toward Zanewna (Zane)'s head then stopped.

Then an older female came over and moved Zanewna (Zane)'s hair so that it was parted revealing the lump on the left side of her head just a little above and behind her ear.

At that point the machines started moving again. The first one seemed to make a cut along the part in the hair that was made for it to follow. At that point it stopped and moved back while the older female came to the table and made another part in Zanewna (Zane)'s hair. Again the robotic arm swung in making another cut. This happened two more times and after the last cut the robotic arm moved out of the way.

At this point the young male moved to the table and with a hand held instrument he separated the scalp from her skull. He laid it gently on the tray beside him then stepped back while another robotic arm swung into place.

I can see all that is happening from where I am glad I am not in Zanewna (Zane)'s body. She seems to be unconscious or I would have been feeling everything. It's all I can do to keep watching but curiosity had taken over and I can't seem to turn away.

"Oh my gosh!" the robotic arm just removed a part of Zanewna (Zane)'s skull and I can see her brain. I have seen pictures of the brain before but it is so much deeper in color than the photos let it be. I am feeling different emotions than I did while looking at the pictures.

I floated in closer to see just what they were doing, after all this is like a once in a lifetime experience.

The robotic arms stopped and moved back and the young male stepped forward to take a closer look. The young female was watching everything on a screen.

"I'm seeing a cerebral contusion. It looks to be eight ttks by fourteen ttks and it looks to be about three ttks deep. So we will have to program to take it out in very thin sheets. Are you seeing it on the viewer?" he asked.

"Yes, I can see it now and I am programing it now." The younger female said.

As he stepped back the robotic arm swung back into place and started to cut the bruised tissue loose while part of it rinsed and vacuumed at the same time.

"Is this want caused her memory loss?" Esentia (Sent) asked the young male.

"Yes, we are pretty sure it was the pressure on the brain from the bruise. After we remove the extra blood and put it all back together I am sure she will remember everything." He assured Esentia (Sent).

"Oh Good." My aunt chimed in. "She is doing some very important experiments.

"Well, I am sure she will be good as new when she wakes up." He said with a smile and slight bow. "I need to finish my job. Thank you" he added as he went back to his place near the machines.

"Okay, I am ready for the skull to be put together again." The young female said looking in his direction as the robotic arm moved back and out of the way.

The second robotic arm moved in and slowly placed the skull piece back in place then rotated out of the way after sealing the skull.

The young male took the tray with Zanewna (Zane)'s scalp and moved in to put it into place so it can be healed.

I am in place so I can see just how these robotic arms work. Zanewna (Zane)'s hair was being held out of the cut areas so what looked like a laser could seal the edges.

"Wow! I'm looking very close and you can't even tell the skin had ever been cut." I reported to Enah 2 (E 2).

"Did you see all that they did to Zanewna (Zane)'s body?" I asked Enah 2 (E 2).

Yes, we had everything shifted to observer." Enah 2 (E 2) answered. "That was both exciting and informative." He added.

"I agree. Are you ready to switch things back the way they were? I think they are getting ready to wake her up." I said.

"We are ready here." He informed me.

About that time the older female walked towards the exam table with a syringe in her hand and I noticed that the floor under her feet turned dark.

She had gotten about half way across the room when the young male noticed and called for intervention. As she got closer to Zanewna (Zane), two men came from out of nowhere it seemed. One of them got to her first and grabbed her arm, but she managed to get loose. I didn't know but the robotic arms around the exam table were programed to protect who or whatever was on the table from harm.

I felt confused at this point how did the robotic arms know the difference between someone helping and someone that intended to do harm?

One of the robotic arms had swung into action and knocked the older female down and both men grabbed her at the same time. And the younger female came forward and took the needle out of the older female's hand.

Zanewna (Zane)'s aunt screamed. "Esentia (Sent)! What is happening?"

"I'm not sure, but I will find out." She answered moving closer to the young male – who was now interrogating the older female.

"It seems that Zanewna (Zane) was working on a project and formula that her nephew was part of and he wanted to take full credit for it. He's the one that cause her to get the head injury." He explained to Esentia (Sent).

Then they both walked over to where Aunt Marzla (Aunt Mars) and explained all of that to her.

"How did you know to stop here?" Aunt Marzla (Aunt Mars) asked.

"Oh that is part of our monitoring system that was installed in our operation rooms a few years back." He explained.

"Monitoring system?" Aunt Marzla (Aunt Mars) and Esentia (Sent) asked almost in unison.

"Yes, it was installed in the floor. That is the reason the floor turns color only under the feet of living beings. You see it monitors our emotions and if the floor turns dark it switched to monitoring the brain waves. Then a panel on monitoring screens sends us an alert and the robotic arms go into protective mode." He explained.

"We heard that and we think that is ingenious." Enah 2 (E 2) said. "The floors are mood detectors with added brainwave reader. I like that idea. That would help in a lot of area here on our own planet." He added.

"Yes, especially where important people were and in interview area." I said with a slight chuckle.

The young male is moving toward Zanewna (Zane) now. He may be ready to wake her up. I am ready to complete my adventure here." I said moving into position.

"Zanewna (Zane), How are you

feeling?" the young male asked.

"I'm feeling a little light headed." I answered after examining and getting a little more oriented with Zanewna (Zane) body again.

"That will soon past. Can you remember anything before you woke up this morning?" He asked, using a light to look at my eyes closer.

"I remember getting hit in the head while at work. And I was writing down what we had done to improve the heat shields." I said slowly examining my memory for more details. Things before that seem to be in fragments." I said.

"Not to worry, all of that will come back together in a few more hours." He assured me with a comforting pat on one shoulder as I got off of the table.

"How soon can I go back to work?" I inquired, while glancing over at my Aunt who was standing near Esentia (Sent).

"I would say give yourself a few more hours. After all you just had brain surgery." He replied with a big smile.

"Ready to go?" Aunt Marzla (Aunt Mars) asked holding, out her hand.

" I guess." I said as Esentia (Sent) walked over to talk to the young male.

"Wait for me at the door," she said loudly toward us.

While we waited my aunt told me all that had happened while I was out.

"Wow, you mean that Jerazal (Zal) wanted all of the credit that bad? That is hard to believe." I said slowly shaking my head.

Esentia (Sent) walked up about that time. "I did find out that you have been cleared to go back to work later today. And that your co-worker Jerazal (Zal) has been taken away and placed in a program that will help him with his problem and that his aunt will be placed in a different program in another canyon some distance from here." She explained as she opened the large blue door.

As we left the doctors group hospital my mind was spinning. New improvements were flying into my mind. I was almost in a run to get back to my aunt's house.

"Slow down Zanewna (Zane), I can't walk that fast. I'm not quite as young as you." She laughed.

"Okay." I said trying to walk slower. But my mind was racing with new ideas that would improve the ideas and ways we already worked it out on the computers at work. And I knew that sometimes flash thoughts were hard to hold on to. Then I remembered about my wrist band having a recorder. So I slowed down and started talking to it, but I was still a little ahead of my aunt.

"What? Zanewna (Zane) what did you say?" Aunt Marzla (Aunt Mars) asked.

"I'm recording Aunt Marzla (Aunt Mars)." I said looking back at her.

I could see she was trying to catch up, and by the time we got to her house she was ahead of me enough to have the door open.

I had been living with her long enough that she recognized the mode of thought I was in. So she didn't bother to say anything to me as I walked passed her to my room.

I had some formulas and drawings I really needed to enter into the computer before I lost the thoughts. The recordings were like highlight thoughts so I wouldn't forget the train of thought I was in at the time.

I had just finished saving all the ideas when I found the edge of a picture sticking out from under a book on my desk. It was a picture of the animal that I saw earlier in the day. I had its name floating in my mind but couldn't quite get it to the front so I could say it out loud. Then I looked at the back of the picture. There it was 'Bluzena' (Blue) that must be my pets name.

Just then she came running through the door making the strange noises she was making earlier. As Zanewna (Zane) I could understand what she was saying. But with my ears all I hear was a very strange growly bark with a couple of squeaks at the end. She was saying the afternoon meal was ready.

As we walked down the long hallway she was explaining that she watched me all night and was worried about me. "Thank you for all of your love and care. I love you too." I said reaching down and giving her a few more pets as we rounder the corner to the large room in the house.

"Enah 2 (E 2) did you have a chance to record all that I put on the computer?" I asked in a whisper.

"Yes and we recorder some history while you were looking at the books earlier. The part about how they mistreated their planet and some of them moved to their moon and how their wars blew it into piece and then their upper atmosphere caught fire and has been burning ever since." He answered.

This all was a surprise to me because I wasn't able to read any of the books. I could only look at the pictures.

"So you can come back any time now." He added.

"Good," I said as I sat back in the soft chair as Zanewna (Zane) and relaxed and soon I was back in the science lab in my chair ready to take off my helmet.

"Wow, that was a lot of information and what an adventure. I had a chance to watch brain surgery." I said, standing up for a good stretch.

"Ok Elaytay (Tay), everything is saved and documented. See you early in the amacron (morning). Okay" Enah 2 (E 2) said.

"Yes sir, some of these can get pretty intense." I said as I walked through the doors.

Chapter Ten
Ice Crossing

It was early in the morning when I walked into the science lab to ask about the assignment for that sestron's (day's) explorations.

"Good morning Enah 2 (E 2). What is on the travel schedule today?" I asked.

"Oh good, Elaytay (Tay). You are right on time. Today your first mission is to visit Strong Bow's home planet and gather the history of his group of people there." Enah 2 (E 2) said greeting be with a big smile.

"It looks like you are going to be finding out more about Earth's history. You will be checking the accuracy of an old Indian legend. I am thinking that it may be one of the stories that Papa Two Wolves may have told you when you first met him and Healing Waters," he said turning to look at me.

Do we know which legend I will be

checking?" I asked while checking my helmet's connections.

"The Science Council named it the "Ice Crossing"," he answered.

'I am hoping I will be there not as part of the group. I heard that a lot of the peoples on that trip didn't make it because of the weather conditions,' I thought, thinking about how cold it is at the North Pole area. "That makes me cold just thinking about it," I said with a shiver.

"Well if your temp drops on this end we will wrap you up and keep you warm," Enah 2 (E 2) said trying to reassure me. "It is time to get started," he added.

I settled back in my chair with my helmet on, took a few deep breaths.

"This time I am caught in what seemed to be a snow storm. I have a sled tied to a harness around my waist and crossing my chest." I whispered into cupped hands toward my ear. "Enah 2 (E 2) can you hear or see what I am seeing?" I asked.

"Yes we are able to see and hear everything you can." Enah 2 (E 2) explained.

"Oh good," I said feeling relieved.

I could barely hear him over the howling winds. But it was enough to let me know he was there.

I looked around me and there was a mixture of people from different parts of the

Earth. Most were rough looking as if they had been working hard all of their lives in outside jobs. I looked at my hands and my skin was of a darker tone like a lot of others. There were a few lighter tones scattered among the different groups. Everyone was trying to keep a steady pace.

'I am hoping that I dropped in on this trip close to the main land mast.' I thought.

Just as that thought passed through my mind I heard some very strange sound, then shortly after that, Chewanee (Chew) came riding by telling everyone to move faster.

Chewanee (Chew) is the leader on this trip. She has made sure we had all of our needs met with warmth and food. But the long walk was starting to wear deeply on everyone. Some have lost family due to age and illness. But she made sure that everyone kept moving forward.

The snow seems to be letting up. I can make out a little piece of blue skies out farther in front of us.

Chewanee (Chew) just went by again pulling a sled full of people that were too weak to keep up with the majority of the group. She was taking them to the front of the group, so they wouldn't be left behind on the ice straits. She would drop them off and repeat her ride down the line of people and pick up the weaker ones. And the whole time now she was telling everyone to move faster now. There was an urgency in her voice.

'I think the loud sounds I heard was the ice starting to crack.' I thought. *'That is scary.'*

As time passed and Enah 2 (E 2) was just watching and hadn't said anything for hours. "I think we are getting close to land now, the snow has let up and the snow isn't as deep. The ice is still really thick and there seems to be new hope in everyone's eyes. And a renewed energy had come over the whole group." I said whispering into cupped hands.

As I took a closer look around at the peoples who followed Chewanee (Chew) on this life changing trip. I could see that there was quite a variety of peoples from all over the Earth.

"We are all safe now. We are on the main land now. And everyone is becoming more relaxed. Groups are starting campfires and warming up. Some have found a warm place and fallen asleep." I whispered to Enah 2 (E 2).

"I can see what you are talking about. But who are those people that are riding towards you on horses?" he asked.

"I'm not sure, Chewanee (Chew) rode out to meet them. I'll see if I can get close enough to hear what's said. I can't get close

enough but, it seems that Chewanee (Chew)
is able to understand and able to
communicate well enough.

Chewanee (Chew) and what seems to
be their main leader are talking and drawing
something in the dirt. She seems to agree and
now she is coming back to our group.

"It seems that there are other groups
already living on this land mass. They are the
children of the ones who landed here a long
time ago. There has been many generation
since their ancestors landed and learned to
live among what they called cave dwellers."
One of them said.

"You are all welcome, the land mast is
large and there are many groups scattered
here." Another one had yelled loudly from a
high rock he was standing on.

All of the peoples that had come on
this trip had managed to break into family
groups and like minded people. So
Chewanee (Chew) is asking that one
representative from each group come
forward so she can explain what she had
been told by the others who already lived
here.

"I am going to try and listen in." I
whispered to Enah 2 (E 2).

Chewanee (Chew) stooped an with a
stick drew the picture she had been shown.

"It seems that these tribal leaders were told by their spirit leaders we were coming. That is why they came to meet us. these are the area that are open to us." she said looking up at the leaders. "How many group leaders are here? Raise your hand." she asked.

Five group leaders raised their hands, the sixth leader spoke up and said, "We choose to stay here in this area."

"Yes, that is good. So in this area, there is room for three groups." She said pointing a large area with a stick.

The group leaders looked at each other and three for them agreed to share the area Chewanee (Chew) was pointing at.

"In this area there is plenty of room for you two leaders and your peoples." She said.

And with that , they nodded in agreement.

"Then is it settled, we will rest here for three days and then each group will take their peoples and head to the areas they have chosen." She said.

She got back on her horse and went back to meet with the leaders that came to meet us and told them that the groups had decided on the areas they had recommended.

"So this is how all the different tribes got here and then made even more tribal groups. That is really nice to see how it all fits together." I said sitting down on a nearby rock.

"Did you hear all of that and did you see the map?" I asked Enah 2 (E 2).

"Yes, and that explained why there are so many tribes and some get upset when others come into their area without permission." He said.

Next thing I knew I was back in the lab taking off my helmet.

What a trip. Cold but informative. I knew that some talked about being her always while others said they came through the ice crossing. So really there are groups that are mixed of both groups. I can hardly wait to let Strong Bow know what I seen today." I said with a big smile.

"Well then we will call it a sestron (day)." Enah 2 (E 2) said with a wave of his hand.

Chapter Eleven
The Shadow Planet

I was glad to see that it was a bright and clear morning. There was no sign of the heavy rain that I had listened to most of the night.

Grams was already up and in the kitchen working on getting breakfast made for all of us. She knew that the council had something new planned for me this morning.

I didn't know much about what they had planned. They had just mentioned that it was something completely different than what we had been doing.

I had to hurry and eat, Time was getting away from me and I didn't want to be late getting to the science labs.

Grams looked up as I came down the stairs to the kitchen. "I hope you are ready to go after you eat. I think all of us are running and little behind our usual times today," she said with a big smile.

"Yes I am ready to leave right after we eat," I said looking around for the rest of the family. "Where is Gramps and Strong Bow? I didn't see them upstairs," I added.

"Yes, well, they were both up early. They are out checking to make sure everything else is ok. That rain last night was the hardest hitting we have had in a very long time," she explained.

Gramps and Strong bow walked through the back door shortly after Grams said that.

"Well, everything seems to have held up pretty well. No one got wet directly. There were a few puddles here and there inside the chicken yard and Notnah (Not) had a small leak in one corner of his place. But Kerzna (Kern) and his family's place is ok," Gramps reported.

"Oh good, well breakfast is on the table, so hurry and wash up so we can all eat before it gets cold," Grams said as she and I sat down.

Elmosa (Mosa) came running through the door just then. "Come look!" he shouted. "You have to see this," he said almost jumping up and down in his excitement.

Gramps and Strong Bow came running back from the bathroom as Grams and I got up. We all met at the back door at the same time.

"What is happening?" Grams asked as she got to the door.

"Well come take a look," Elmosa (Mosa) said standing in the yard and pointing at the sky. "You have to come out here to see it," he exclaimed.

Gramps had made it out to where Elmosa (Mosa) was standing.

"Oh! Well that is something we don't see all of the time," he said with a chuckle.

"What?" Grams asked again as she got to where they were standing.

"A triple rainbow Grams. Just look isn't that awesome?" Elmosa (Mosa) said still excited about being the first one to see it.

"Now that is a site to behold," Grams said.

"We all stood there for a few more microns (seconds) before Grams announced that breakfast was getting cold and we all had things to do today.

"Yes, I only have a short time before going on a special trip today. I wasn't told much except it was going to be different and an experiment," I said while turning to walk back into the house.

Strong Bow caught up with me and gave me a hug and kiss before I sat down. "Good morning love," he said with a big grin.

"Good morning to you too. I will be

back as soon as I get through with whatever we are doing today," I said following it with another kiss.

"It seems that all of the guys plan to go fishing today," Grams said looking at Gramps and almost laughing.

Breakfast was over and I needed to head out the door.

"Wait!" Strong Bow said while catching up with me. "I'll walk a short distance with you then catch up with Gramps and the rest of the group."

"Who all are going fishing this sestron (today)?" I asked.

"Oh Gramps, myself, Elmosa (Mosa), Kerzna (Kern) and Notnah (Not)," he informed me.

"I can see where that may be a lot of fun," I said almost laughing.

"Love you hun, but I had better head back and catch the others," he said giving me another kiss and hug.

"Bye," I said with a wave.

It didn't take long for me to get to the science lab.

"Good amacron (morning) Enah 2 (E 2)," I said as I walked through the lab door.

"Oh hello Elaytay (Tay), are you ready for today's adventure?" he asked.

"I hope so. What are we doing this sestron (today)? I was told very little, just that we were going to try something different than what we normally do," I said, while Enah 2 (E 2) went through the check list of equipment on the clipboard in his hand at the time.

"We are going to try a future view," he said while adjusting the dials of one of the control panels.

"The future? What planet?" I asked.

"The council decided to take a look at Strong Bows planet. The one he named Earth," Enah 2 (E 2) said looking very serious in my direction.

"Well we have been looking at this planet on two of my journeys so far," I said. "But I don't mind, it is a very interesting planet," I added.

"Ok, finish getting prepared. We are scheduled to start at 0700," he informed me.

That gave me roughly fifteen keptrons (minutes) to get everything prepared.

"Okay, everything is in place," I said as I put on my helmet and sat down to relax.

The last thing I saw before closing my eyes was Enah 2 (E 2) and two other science technicians at the consoles making adjustments. There had never been a future exploration before this.

"Enah 2 (E 2), can you hear me ok?" I asked

His voice came in clear but very faint.

I was keeping my hopes up that this all turns out okay.

"All we can see is darkness. What is happening?" he asked.

"Your voice is very faint. Can you speak louder?" I asked. "I'm caught in dark gray swirling clouds or mist. I'm not able to see anything yet." I added.

"Keep me posted. Let me know when things change. We will know then if we need to make adjustments." Enah 2 (E 2) said.

His voice was a little louder but not by much.

"There seems to be a break in the clouds just ahead of me. I seem to be suspended above the Earth. I think I'm about… a one half mile or maybe a little more," I reported.

"What are you seeing?" Enah 2 (E 2) asked.

"Well what I can see of it… it looks like a war zone. But the sky is hard to see through. It is a dark dusky orange and very polluted and the smell is very bad. I don't know how long I will be able to stay here. I'm not sure what form I am in, first hand or observer?" I said. "There are large craters as if it's all been bombed. There are still explosions going off," I added.

I paused and looked around me. It is getting a little lighter behind me but the clouds are still swirling.

"I'm going to try a few things and see what happens," I reported.

I stretched out my hand very slowly toward the Earth and I started to move closer and when I pulled my hand back, I stopped moving. But now I was close enough to see movement below.

Then I heard something behind me. I turned to look as quick as I could move, which seemed to be very slow. I got turned just enough to see a bright being standing close by. I can't make out its face so I have no idea if it is a male or female.

"I am one of the guardian of this area." the guardian explained.

"Can you explain what you are seeing or doing? I am not able to see or hear at this point," Enah 2 (E 2) said clearly.

"I found out I can move a little by pointing my hand. But now there is a very bright being coming closer to me. And there is a soft humming in the background," I said. "I can hear its voice even though I haven't seen any movement. I think it communicates telepathically," I added.

"In that case you will need to repeat what it says, so I will know what is going on," Enah 2 (E 2) said, sounding very interested.

"This is near the end of the planet you

know as Earth. She had gotten sick from all of the pollutions, mistreatment and negative energy of humankind. She is getting ready to shed her third dimensional form in order to move to the next realm. She will leave all of the chaos, illness and negative energy behind" the guardian said.

I quickly repeated the message to Enah 2 (E 2) as it looked at me, seemingly to understand what I was doing.

I guess I looked a little confused. Because I was given the answer to the questions before I was able to ask them.

"Yes, everything in the third realm is what you know as a physical body. And it is time for her to be reborn into the next higher realm," it related to me. *"Wait and you will see what I mean,"* the guardian added.

"I am waiting to see the Earth reborn. It is dying in the third dimension because of all the pollution and other things it has been put through," I reported.

I was going to ask for the guardian to tell me more about what made the Earth sick but before I could physically ask, I was told. *"The Earth got sick because of man's greed and wastefulness, not caring what they did to the Earth as long as they got what they wanted at the time. Pollution and negative thoughts and actions made the whole Earth toxic. This is not to say that there are those who have tried to hold positive thoughts but there became so few that the negative over took her health. Those of positive thoughts and good hearts will be changed along with her and taken into the next realm. Just watch."*

"I will have more information for you in a little bit," I reported to Enah 2 (E 2).

We seemed to back away from the Earth and I could see the whole Earth cleared now since I was no longer in the pollution. At the same time I was given two views of the Dying Mother Earth. I could see a close up of two people working side by side in a bubble. It was like seeing the whole view of the same thing and at the same time seeing a close up side by side.

There was a great groaning and then I could see what almost looked like an eclipse. There was a new Earth coming from out of the darkened pollution of her sick and dying form. It was bright and clear. At the same time Mother Earth was being reborn, one of the two people working on the sick dyeing Earth started to fade from sight of the other worker. Leaving the one left behind looking around for the person that had transcended the sick Earth to the reborn healthy Earth.

I was drawn closer so I could behold all that is now as it was in her perfect form. The sky is bright and clean the clouds are whites like fluffy cotton, the air smelled fresh and the sweetness of flowers wafted through the air. The streams looked like clear glass and sparkled as if small diamonds were rolling across the colored stones. The taste of the clean water was indescribable. All of the animals I could see where happy and healthy and getting along. The people were happy working in their fields and there was energetic singing as they worked. You could feel the love for what they were doing. The plants were all standing tall as if proud to be where they were.

I turned to say what I thought of the things I was seeing. As I turned I was met with a large smile. *"Yes, this is the way it will be in this realm. And this will last for a very long time according to man's years,"* the guardian said.

"I was just shown a new Earth. It was born or I should say birthed from the old sick Earth. I'm not sure what happened to the sick Earth right now. I haven't seen it since the rebirth happened. But the new healthy Earth is perfect in all areas," I reported.

"You are wondering about what happened to the sick polluted Earth in the third dimension and the peoples that were left there." The guardian said. *"All that were of a negative thought pattern were left in their place on the dead Earth. I will take you there and let you see all there is."*

I nodded and with the wave of its hand we were back suspended above the sick

Earth. Then we started to get closer and I
could see more and more of it.

"Oh my gosh, what horrors," I said
aloud.

"What?" Enah 2 (E 2) asked.

"I'm looking at the dead Earth. There
were burned out buildings and some were
falling down. It looked like they had been
bombed and the pollution was so bad it was
hard to see over a couple of blocks away from
where you were standing. Then I saw some
of the people. They were sick with soars all
over their bodies. Like that from radiation
burns. Some had skin just barely holding on,
most of their hair was missing and some you
could even see their bones. They looked like
they should have been dead, but they were
still walking around as if nothing had
happened to them. Some looks like they
should be dead, with body parts just barely
attached, throats cut, heads half bashed in. It
was as if all of the horror that physical beings
have ever thought of had come to pass. I
looked over my shoulder at the being
standing nearby and we were whisked away
to another area, where there should have
been plants and trees, but there wasn't any.
The plants were all dead and where there
were supposed to be trees were just stumps.
They had all been cut down and the water
was polluted with the bodies of dead animals

and bloated fish that had died before the new birth." I reported to Enah 2 (E 2).

I looked over and the being. *"I needed to know why."*

'This is the planet of those who thought they were in power and that only their little world was important. Now they have inherited it completely. There is no death for those who are left, no matter how hard they try. Their negative thoughts have created the world they desired. They will remain alive standing on the end of days,' the guardian related to me straight into my mind. Then the guardian asked *"Have you seen enough?"*

"Is there a date in our time for all of this?" I asked.

"Sooner than most have planned, but only the Holy Creator knows the time," came the answer loud and clear.

I had just finished saying "Yes I have seen enough, Thank you." When the clouds started swirling around me again as it did in the beginning.

I worked at relating all that I had seen to Enah 2 (E 2) as the clouds swirled.

Then as suddenly as it had all started I was seemingly dumped back in my seat holding onto my helmet.

As I opened my eyes, all I could say was "Wow what a wild ride!"

Enah 2 (E 2) gave a laugh. "We

couldn't see much at most points so you will need to draw some of the things you seen, or maybe explain to one of our artist."

"Not a problem it is well ingrained. I don't think I will be able to forget what I have seen," I said getting up to go to the art area of the lab.

"It may be quicker if I just describe what I saw to the computer and let it draw the pictures," I informed Enah 2 (E 2).

"Yes that may go faster," he agreed.

Chapter Twelve
The Pyramid Builders

"Hello Enah 2 (E 2)." I said flinging open the lab door. I seem to have a lot of energy and a little more strength than usual.

"Well, hello. You must have had a good sleep. It seems you are ready to start since you are in your seat already." Enah 2 (E 2) laughed.

"Yes where am I going this sestron (day)?" I asked putting on my helmet.

"The council has requested information about the origin of pyramids." Enah 2 (E 2) said.

"Ok, let's go find out what we can. I love this job, it's sort of addicting." I said with a big smile, laying back to relax.

I was awakened by a loud clatter and angry screaming voices. It seems that my Aunt had come over to argue with my Father again. The kingdom had been passed to my Father, King Potastya (Pots) because he was good at heart and seen that trading with other planets was good for all. As long as greed didn't enter the equation everyone was a winner. This was the way my grandfather ran things and we had always had a peaceful life, except for when my aunt got a bug under her crown and would come over to raise trouble with my father. She had a son who was always spending their wealth as if it was easy to come by and thought everything was to be handed to him without effort on his part. After his allowance was spent he would demand more. Which in turn would get my aunt needing more and more and that is what the argument was about again this morning.

"Enah 2 (E 2), Can you hear and see everything okay?" I asked. I wasn't sure if I would be able to fill him in on what was happening like I had at other times.

"Yea, everything is coming in great." He replied quickly.

I seemed to know all that was needed in this visit.

My father was one that thought the children should be taught how to handle what they get and make it last as long as they could. They were to learn how to save some for the bigger things they wanted. If by chance they needed more, then they were to work for it. All of us, my older and younger brothers and myself, all had jobs to do for our allowance and Dad had told my aunt that her son, Geecrawbee (Craw), should be treated the same as us. Dad said "He hadn't just been given money for sitting around, and he couldn't see giving her any more than what Grandfather had laid out in his instructions before he passed into the next realm."

We are known all over as being the pyramid builders. Our family has been in control of these charging stations for many generations. Not to say that there hasn't been a few groups that have tried their hand at it, but they didn't work as well. We had started from our home planet which is a short distance from the polar star in this galaxy and worked our way toward other solar systems. It seems to make travel a little easier if one didn't have to worry about running out of power or having a place for rest and recreation. We never charged for the use of the stations, it was trades made by each planetary group.

On the other hand my aunt wants to take over and wants her son to be king. He doesn't know anything about the charging stations or about how the trading works. He just wants to get more riches. Even if he had all of the riches in the universe he would have nothing in a matter of a very short time.

The kingdom is set up right now for my older brother, Jawnobee (Nobee), to take over if something was to happen to my father. Our peoples live for a very long time. The average is about four hundred years. My older brother is nearly an adult now and I am what would be known as a preteen and my younger brother is still a very young child.

My aunt finally went back to her kingdom, and the rest of the day went along as peacefully as expected.

Later that evening we all sat down and ate dinner and afterward we were all served a very delicious dessert. After we ate it, we were told that it was from my aunt as an apology for acting the way she had earlier. We sat and talked for a while about the next charging stations that was planned and the improvements to be made and then we all said our good nights and went to bed.

Morning came early with loud weeping. I got dressed quickly to find out what had happened. That is when I found out that my father had died during the night. I thought that was very strange because he was in great health.

Traditions said that the late king had

to be present when the new king was crowned and so Jawnobee was crowned by noon.

Geecrawbee (Craw) pitched a tantrum saying it wasn't fair because he was older than my brother. And that the charging station should be selling the power and not just trading it for other goods. And if he was king he would sell the power and sell the goods he did get in trade. That would mean that the people that used the goods would not have them until they could manage to get the amount Geecrawbee (Craw) was asking for them.

Jawnobee didn't get to be king for long, just a matter of a few months before he was killed. My younger brother was too young to rule and I protested the idea of making Geecrawbee (Craw) king. I knew he would make hard for everyone he ruled over to live like they were used to. They would all become his slaves.

My mother screamed, "Zeeknonobee (Zeek), don't protest. You know what will happen,"

Enah 2 (E 2) whispered in my ear, "Be careful of what you say or do."

But I felt I had to protest for the peoples and the kingdom's sake.

My father had made sure to have burial pyramids build for each of us using his own design. He used to tell me that pyramids held a special power of their own and if built right their energy would help you into the next level.

'Well, I did protested and when Geecrawbee (Craw) becoming king I have been sentenced to be buried alive with my brother in his death vault,' I fought as strongly as I could.

"I and my younger brother are in the vault with Jawnobee (Nobee) and they are getting ready to close the door. Can you hear me?" I asked hoping to get an answer from Enah 2 (E 2).

"Yes I am getting all of the information you have sent. But it is getting hard at times to make it all out, like now. The vault may be interfering," he said in a lower volume than usual.

The door slammed and I heard the lock drop into place.

A panic set in. 'Oh my God there isn't much air in the chamber. We may only have a few hours at most. I don't want to die like this. I really want to see my family again. Oh please be able to hear me.' I don't want to say it all out loud because that would use what little air that is in the chamber.

I could hear Bennobee (Ben) trying to hold back tears. "Don't worry Bennobee

(Ben) we will get out of here. Relax and let me think." I said quietly.

"Ok" he whispered. "I will think too."

"Dad always said "Two bright minds have a better chance of getting a great answer." I added.

I decided to lie back against the wall and close my eyes. My mind started to wonder back through my life of all of the things I had done and seen. Thoughts of my family and their friends and the work I had done and the things I had helped discover and it wasn't too bad. I had done a lot and seen plenty but I was still in hopes that Enah 2 (E 2) would figure a way out to get me home again.

Then all of a sudden I was jolted out of deep thought by a loud sliding noise and then a deep sounding thud. It sounded like one of the stones had fallen. I got up and looked around the room. I didn't see anything out of place. Then I looked up.

"I just moved a few things." Bennobee (Ben) said shyly.

Then I looked up. "Oh my gosh! There is a tunnel in the ceiling and I can see a star peeking though at me.

They had left a torch burning for us when they locked us in here and I just noticed that there was plenty of furniture to pile onto different pieces to get one of us to the opening in the ceiling. At least we knew we would have air. There just might be a way that I could climb out of here; after all I am pretty slim. I have to try. We started putting more pieces of furniture on top of each other and then climbing up to reach the tunnel.

'Dang not enough yet and that seems to be all there is. There has to be a way. If I step back into that corner maybe an idea will come. It took a few minutes of refiguring it all in my head but I think I have it. But it meant taking it all down and piling it all back in a different order. I'm sure I have it,' I thought as I climbed up all of the pieces with the last piece in my hands.

'Just enough for me to get a good hold on the inside of the tunnel. It took a while for me to wiggle my way to the top but I was out of the pyramid and I was really close to the top. It was dark and no one could see me.

"Enah 2 (E 2) can you hear me now," I asked. I waited to hear something before I started the climb down the back side of the pyramid, but I didn't hear anything.

I managed to find some clothes that had been left on a line outside. I changed and buried my other clothes. After hunting for a short time I found some rope and hurried back to help Bennobee (Ben) out of the pyramid.

The next morning at daylight I found a band of traders headed to the outer moon. We joined them and were free.

I managed to find a private area and tried again to reach Enah 2 (E 2). "Can you hear me? Enah 2 (E 2) please answer me," I begged.

"Oh good, yes I can hear you now. We had some problems with one of the circuits and it was down for a while. Are you ready to come home?" he asked.

"Yes more than ready, Bennobee (Ben) is safe and I have memorized where all of the energy stations are located," I said glad to hear his voice.

I lay back against the wall of the ship and relaxed. The next thing I knew Enah 2 (E 2) was taking the helmet off of me.

"Boy, am I glad to be home. I don't know what you heard last but I remember it all very well. I thought I was going to suffocate before I could escape the burial vault," I said excited to be back.

"What burial vault, yes we missed all of that. You will need to tell all of us what happened. After your brother was killed," Enah 2 (E 2) said.

So I sat there in the science time lab and explained all that happened on this trip before leaving to go home that ponacron (evening). But the main thing I wanted to let him know was the charging station pyramid locations. Their planet is in the same galaxy as Strong Bows and is the point of light just beyond Cassiopeia's foot or the head of the Elk Skin as know by Papa Two Wolves. They had managed to place pyramids on almost every planet and some moons between their planet and Earth.

Chapter Thirteen
I knew you before

"Hello Enah 2 (E 2)? Anyone here, Hello" I said as loud as I dared without screaming. *'Well that is odd. I'm on time. I wonder where everyone is.'*

'Well I'm going to sit down and relax. I will put on my helmet and just be ready to go to work when they do finally get here. Just relax and see where I end up.

This must be a dream or am I traveling? Just go with it and see where it leads.'

I am a young five year old girl playing with my doll at the back of our trailer. I'm having a tea party with my dolls when all of a sudden....

This is very strange. Where is everything? All I see is white. I don't want to move, I may fall from where ever I am. I'm just going to sit here and look around. But there is nothing to look at, it's all bright white. I'm not in a fog because I can see my hands. I know fog because my dad has pulled our trailer through it before. At least that is what mom and dad called it. But this is even whiter than fog.

Just then I felt the presents of a person. Do I look or just keep my head down. Then I saw the sandals and feet of a person.

I have the feeling of being safe and as I look up I see a very tall person. I'm feeling safer and calm. He put out his hand for me to take it and so I did. He helped me to my feet and we just stood there for a few minutes. He had a very loving look on his face and was dressed like the guys I had remembered seeing in the bible stories my mom and grandma would read to me every night. He had on a long robe with an orange and gold sash. His hair was shoulder length and golden brown and there was a bright white light showing around him.

I'm not sure where we went or how long I was gone. But from that time, I have been asked question about other things like time and dimensional shifts and matters of spirit and I somehow knew the answers.

I was brought back from where ever I was to the here and now of my consciousness and my dolls.

I have gone through so many near

death experiences and traveled beyond reality as commonly known since then.

But I did find out later that I was free to travel were ever in time, space and dimensionally anytime I needed or wanted to. I was only limited to where I desired to be at the time.

But I remember seeing and doing things in that the time realm that seemed strange to me when I came back to my doll.

What we call modern times now are just now thinking of experimenting with, doing or even finding out about things that in some ways have already happened.

Chapter Fourteen

Another Space / Time/ Dimensional Shift

I came into the lab on my day off because Enah 2 (E 2) and I had talked about traveling on our own time.

I sat down in the chair. I didn't put on the helmet because I didn't want to go to a preprogramed time or place.

I sat down and started my meditational breathing and the next thing I remember was being about five years old and a ship landed in our yard of my mom's parent's house. Van and a friend got out and Van and I talked for a long time. He and his friend would come to visit whenever they had a chance for the next seventeen years. Van was from a planet that was very far away but I never really asked him which one because I really didn't care. He was dressed in a silver metallic jump suit that seemed to zip up the front with a colored V that went up and around his neck with the point in front. He was my friend and I didn't have many.

My family (my parents and my dad parents) traveled a lot for work. Grandpa was a pipefitter and my dad was a boom operator.

Van just said "I can't be seen by anyone here or at least very few on your plane. That didn't bother me any because I had a friend that no matter where we moved, Van always knew where to find me.

Somehow I skipped forward in time and I'm older and I didn't see Van very often, but once in a while he would come and talk for a little while then take off again.

Now I'm an adult and was married. Van came one evening and found me sitting out on my front porch looking up at the stars. We talked for a while about the things that had been happening in our lives and then before he left he said "I will see you in five years in physical form."

I remember thinking that was a little odd but didn't think any more about it.

Time went by and in the next time jump, I'm giving birth to a son and somehow I knew it was Van and I knew in my heart of hearts that he was only going to be here for a short while.

He once told me, "Life is like being in school. There were lessons to learn and projects to complete in order to graduate to the next level."

I remember taking this as part of the lessons he needed to complete to get to the next level. I'm thinking that maybe he needs to be physical to learn the lesson in this realm/grade.

Time went by and he had to have shots in order to go to school but every time we went to the doctors or hospital he would almost go into hysterics. He would scream as if he was in pain or so frightened that it was hard to keep him from running.

One evening, while sitting on the front step and singing a song. The words and melody were strange and I seem to be making it all up as I sing it. The song is talking about coming here for a short visit to experience life and learning the lessons well. Passing the tests and moving on but only being here for a short while.

Then one day he was playing with some of the other children in the area and fell from an old shed about twelve foot. He didn't break anything, but my grandma said she wanted the doctor to check him for leukemia, he was showing the same signs I did when I had it.

The doctor at the clinic refused to do the blood test and I tried several time to get his to do the test and was refused every time. This discussion went on for several visits/months. He said, "You are just paranoid because your daughter was just diagnosed with type one diabetes. There is no need for any test on your son."

My grandma said "When you had leukemia you fainted the same way and so I want you to take him to my doctor because he is willing to do the test."

Before I could get from the town she lived in back to my house the results of the tests were back. He did have leukemia.

This didn't really surprise me because I knew he was just here long enough to gain all of the experiences he needed before leaving.

I went back to my doctor and told him that he may want to run the test or I would have to get a lawyer. He ran the test and they started treatment, but by this time a good nine months had past.

During that time I had continued my practices of meditation and prayers. I knew that there was a lot more to life than the average human could ever dream of and that for some reason when anyone asked me a question about something I somehow knew the answer.

I felt like I was living other lives at the same time I was living the one here on this planet. But I was told at a very early age, mum is the word because if you were to try and explain this to the average person they would see that you were put away and medicated. So I never talked to anyone about it. But I would have visions and knew that the angel or the strange being that took me by the hand when I was younger taught me a lot of things that I needed to understand later in this life.

The doctors started my son on all of their meds and did their treatments for what seemed a life time. But it was only for about five years.

At one point he had what the doctor call seed warts covering the bottoms of both feet. The doctor gave me a lotion and a roll of clear tape to wrap his feet in once I put the lotion on. It was to cause blister and cause the warts to fall off. To me that seemed like more pain than was needed.

I never used the lotion because I was told a safer and less painful way to clear them up.

So I taught my son a meditation that would clear the virus that was causing the warts and in about three days his feet were clear. While all of this was going on, I was carrying my son out to the freeway ramp to catch rides into San Francisco for his treatments. One day I leaned him against a post on the entrance ramp and put up my thumb to catch a ride. He had to see the doctor in San Francisco every day.

One day while holding out my thumb, after leaning my son against a nearby post. A car drove up partway onto the medium

where I was standing and the guy pulled out
a gun and pointed it at my son. I jumped in
between him and my son. "STOP!" I yelled in
the most powerful voice I could find. The
guy pulled the gun back in and they raced
away. I found out later that the voice I had
used was called a power voice.

When we went back to the doctor on
the third day his feet were clear. He thought
it was his meds that did the trick until I told
him what we had been doing.

A little more time went by and my son
started limping and one arm started drawing
up tighter to his chest and he started to drool.
The doctor it looked like and said there were
tumors forming above his left ear in the
temple area of his brain and he wanted to
place him on even more medications. I said
let me try one thing for about a week before
you decide that is the way to go and he
agreed, after all the feet had cleared up and
he had no explanation for that.

So I took my son home and told him,
"Think of your brain as being like one of the
old jukeboxes, like in the movies with all of
the records standing upright. The first record
has gotten scratched up really bad and isn't
worth keeping. So see yourself tossing that
record out and playing the next one. After all
that record has the same songs without any
scratches." He did this during a meditation
and in two days the limp was gone, his arm

was back right again and there was no drooling. His doctor was totally surprised and didn't know what to say.

As time passed he was in and out of the hospital. We continued our meditations even in the hospital. Then one day during meditation I found myself floating in a special place that I came to called The Crystal City, because of the way it looked. There were very large buildings that shone as if they were made of the most precious gemstones and metal. The sky was made of white mother of pearl. The stream that flowed through the city was so clear and pure beyond words. The blades of grass and the flowers sparkled as if made of purest most precious rhinestones. There were children playing and laughing among what we would consider wild and dangerous animals. I got to know my way around the city and knew a lot of the guardians and gained even more information. They were dressed a lot like the person that I had seen when I was five.

One of the guardians gave me a warning right off, "Don't touch anything while you are here. If you want a door opened or a book opened then ask and we will do it for you. If you touch anything at this point you will be required to stay." I found out later that this place is like a holding center for those between lives. The more time I spent there learning the more I understood about how things worked. All I can say is that there is so much more going on behind the scenes, than the average human could ever imagine.

My son and I would meditate together. He had been taught what is called active meditation by one of the groups we attended at the time.

My son's immune system started to fail and the doctor put him in the hospital in what was called ICU at this point he had come down with complications and now had I.V.'s in both arms and couldn't eat because of the blisters in his mouth. He had always told me that when he got grown he wanted to design and test pilot flying sauces. I always told him I thought he was a little ahead of schedule for that. This world wasn't ready for those yet.

It became easier for me to talk to the guardians of the Crystal City and I found out that they had set up a place that looked exactly like the hospital room here in our physical realm. My son also knew not to touch anything while in The Crystal City and was smart enough not to touch anything while he was there, that way he could come back here to our physical realm.

Well it soon got to the point when it was time for my son to leave this realm, but he didn't want to leave because he was afraid for me and his sisters. He was in so much pain and his body was so swollen from the medication and it hurt just to swallow from all of the blisters in his mouth and throat. He was still determined to make people laugh. He had learned how to paint pictures with his feet. I would tape a brush to his big toe.

We visited The Crystal City daily during our joined meditations. The guardian wanted to take him home but couldn't talk him into touching anything while he was there.

After the pain got so bad that the meds couldn't block it any more, I finally gave permission to the guardians to trick him. I watched all of this during one of our joined meditations one day.

'They took him on a trip to what he thought was The City but they had really gone out far enough to make a large U-turn and came back here to our physical realm. He refused to touch anything here but when he left here he though we was coming back to the physical world. I was sitting next to the bed when he gave one last cough and a little blood came from his mouth. He called and I could see him trying to move the physical body but it had already gotten stiff. He was allowed to come back just enough to talk telepathically to me one last time for about two min from the spirit realm. I could hear him and see him because of the way I was raised. He needed to know that we would all be ok and I assured him that we would all be ok.

"Elaytay (Tay)" I heard Enah 2 (E 2) voice in my ear. "I didn't know you had come in. Is everything ok?" he asked

It took me a few microns (seconds) to gather my thoughts and come back from where ever I had gone. "Yes I'm ok. I have been having the strangest dream."

"Yes, I see you have." He said with a light chuckle.

"What do you mean?" I asked

"Well a while back we made the chair so that it starts recording within microns (seconds) of anyone sitting down in it.

"Oh my goodness, so all of that is recorded?" I ask just to make sure I had heard him right.

"Yes, right here." he said holding up a small discnod (memory disc).

I was just thinking back on the idea of us being able to time travel. I am wondering if what I just experienced was sort of a cross into a part of me that is living in a different dimension or realm." I said, just sort of throwing out an idea.

I hadn't really thought about that much. But since times and consciousness is up to the perceiver, I don't see why it couldn't be just that.

You know that thought opens up a whole new concept. And that opens a whole new area of questions, like. When we time travel, how do we know we are getting the information from our timeline and not from a different reality?

I will have to check with our others research team and see if they can give us an answer." He said with a big smile.

I think that may keep them wondering for a while. After all how would you be able to prove that one way or the other?

Chapter Fifteen
"Who is the Real Ghost?"

Right before I left the time chamber sacytron (yesterday), Enah 2 (E 2) had mentioned something about exploring different dimensions.

Looking at my timelink "Oh my, if I don't hurry I will be late meeting up with Enah 2 (E 2)". I shouted on my way down the stairs.

Strong Bow met me on the main floor, "Then you had better hurry, Love" he said reaching out to give me a kiss and a huge hug. "Be safe and hurry home, but have fun this sestron (day)."

My excitement gained momentum as I headed for the Science Center. As I opened the large doors I was greeted by Enah 2 (E 2). "Come on in. We have a lot to go over before we start this sestron (today)" he said as he motioned for me to follow him.

"We think we have found a way into other dimensions. We have found that everything created everywhere is connected, not only in this space and time but all of them." he said giving the gesture to everything in sight

"You said everything created. You mean everything including things like these machines, buildings and all." I said figuring to rule out a few things.

"No, but everything that has life, and that is naturally made by The Creator, and nature or made from natural materials" he explained. "That's not to say that if you were to travel to another timeline that has another part of yourself in it that you would not see a lot of the same things you have here in this one. If fact the only difference you may find is that you are either ahead or behind in the things you have done or planning to do. And there may be a few things in different places, but outside of that you would think you were here in your own time." he continued. "Unless there was a major different decision made in life that wasn't necessary in your life here." he added.

"You mean we have learned how to travel not only in time but in different dimensions now?" I asked, fascinated with the thought.

"Well it isn't as much of a different dimension as it is time and places. Some areas times moves faster or slower than our own and in some places there doesn't seem to be time at all, in the places where there doesn't seem to be time we have named them timeless dimensions."

he explained.

"Okay, well that would make sense, and helps to keep them apart, at least in my head." I said with a laugh.

"Are you ready?" He asked pointing at the chair.

"Yes!" I answered.

I sat down in my chair and put the helmet on and started my breathing exercises.

"How long will I be gone? I asked wondering if I would be home in time for dinner.

"I will send you out on a short trip to start with. You will be in the other time line for about a decon (hour), but will be back here in about 10 keptrons (minutes)." He instructed. "You will just be an invisible observer this time." he added.

"Close your eyes." he instructed. "Keep them closed till the flashing has stopped." he added.

"Flashing?" I asked.

"Yes, In some dimensional spaces there are flashes, some very bright and some a little dimmer, we think they are like time clicks, you know sort of like divisions of time, like sestrons (days), pestrons (weeks) or mistrons (months) etc." he explained.

"Oh, Okay. How long do I wait after the last flash before opening my eyes." I asked.

"Count to 10, I think that will be enough." Enah 2 (E 2) explained. "Ok eyes closed, here you go. Oh! Almost forgot when we get ready to bring you back, it will seem like the lights get dimmer. At that point relax and close your eyes again" he added.

"Ok" I said leaning back and closed my eyes, in a matter of microns (seconds) it seemed there were a lot of fast flashes then they started slowing down but there were still only a few microns (seconds) between them. Then the last one came, I waited for a few microns (seconds) before I started my counting. I opened my eyes, but it didn't seem that I had gone anywhere except that I didn't feel like I had the helmet on anymore. I looked around and everything was just the same, except I was standing on the street leading to Grams house. So I went home. As I walked up the steps to the porch I could smell a great meal cooking. I went to an opened the door and my hand went through the handle. I walked through the screen door, no one seemed to notice me as I walked into the kitchen and dinner was almost ready, the bread had been pulled out of the oven to cool and the roast was being basted for the last time, potatoes were being mashed and the salad was already on the table. I could smell fresh peach pie. But then I started to look around the room, there were a few things that were in different places. The clock was on the other side of the family picture. And in the picture where Kerzna (Kern) was to be, there was another strange looking animal instead. And after a second look Grams kitchen table wasn't wood it looked to be made of something else, just not sure what. Grams went to the back door and rang the bell for supper. Gramps came in first, he looked a little different, his hair seemed a little darker. Strong Bow came in next after dusting off his pants. He had longer hair and it was in a braid in back. Then Elmosa (Mosa) and my other self-came in from another room. Elmosa (Mosa) was wearing a headband like his dad and my hair was lighter in color. But everyone acted the same. Strangely enough, no one could see me and yet I was able to eat some of the food without any of it missing.

After everyone finished eating, my other self-walked down the short hall leading to the living room with me trailing. We passed a mirror and I could see both of us. I guess she saw both of us too. She stopped and looked at me a little closer. My reflection looked as if it was in a light fog.

"Are you real? she asked looking right at me.

"Yes, but I think I am in another dimension," I replied. "Has Cyterrious (Ci-tear-ious) started doing time travel yet?" I asked.

Just as she started to answer the lights seemed to dim and then got bright again. I sat down in the nearest chair and relaxed. The next thing I knew Enah 2 (E 2) was touching me on the hand saying. "Your back, how did it go?"

"It went real good as far as I could tell.

There were differences that I noticed." I said relating to him where I went, and what all had changed.

"So now you had a chance to see what I was talking about, the small changes that one wouldn't normally notice unless you are really looking for them. Some places in time there are even fewer changes. We still have a lot of studies to do yet dealing with the mind and consciousness. But I have an idea that we can travel to these other areas in time if but only a very short time, humankind that is." Enah 2 (E 2) explained while looking over at me with a slight smile.

"Why do you say that?" I asked.

"I have over-heard a few people in the past saying that they just knew that they had place an object in a special place and when they went back for it, it was gone. But then they would walk out of the room and right back into that room and the object would be right where they thought they had left it. So far I have only heard two explanations for such happenings. One is time slippage where a person's becomes conscious in another time for a few microns (seconds) and the other is that of fairies and gnomes making things unseen for a little while to get attention. Both right off seem a little strange. I am waiting to see which one wins. Or maybe it is a combination of both, wouldn't that be wild." He explained almost sounding intrigued.

"Wow what a thought. I mean us being able to do something like that without all this equipment.

"I think we will call it a day and start on the real testing tostron (tomorrow)." Enah 2 (E 2) announced pointing toward the door.

"Oh I totally agree. In the amacron (morning) then, see you then." I said as I gave a short wave and started home.

As I got closer to Grams house it seemed lighter in color than before. Then I thought back, in the other time frame Grams house was just slightly darker in color than here.

"Wow! What a trip. I guess there are things that you wouldn't normally notice." I muttered to myself as I walked up the front steps.

"Hi everyone, I'm home." I shouted as I walked into the house.

"Oh, Good, I'm in the kitchen. Come tell me how it all went and what you found out." came Grams' voice from the kitchen.

It was getting close to dinner and I could smell…. a roast?

"Grams what are we having for dinner tonight?" I called out as I walked towards the kitchen.

"A roast and all the trimmings." came her answer. I come in and set down and tell me all that happened today. she continued.

I sat down and proceeded to tell Grams

everything that had happened that day. She listen very intently and even stopped what she was doing to ask questions.

Then she added…"You do know that there are other realms where the fairies and gnomes live along with all that we call fantasy folk and they have known for a very long time how to slip in and out of our realm. You know I think that at one point in time all of the realms were able to visit one another at will, then something happened and we, humans, weren't able to travel in and out of time like we use to. I have always wondered what happened that locked that door." she added with a far-away look.

"But, I was wondering, when the times and dimensions come that close to each other and we see the people or things in that other area, are they the ghost or are we?" I asked.

"I think that thought may go both ways. I mean wouldn't we be each other's ghost?" gram answered. "But you do know there is a difference between time realms and dimensions? But that is a discussion for another time. Right now it's time to set the table and get everyone cleaned up for dinner." she said while looking over her shoulder with a big smile.

Other Books
by
Lauresa Tomlinson

Chapter Books
Elaytay (Tay)'s Adventures in Space and Time
Pt 1- We Came to Visit
Pt 2 We Meet at Last

Crazy déjà vu (pt-1)
Crazy déjà vu - Not Again (pt-2)

My Interview With a Fairy
The Turning Stone
Secretly Special – You Maybe Special Too
There's an Alien in My Cereal
Magic Under the Pear Tree

Picture Books
Munchie & Goldie – Most Unlikely Friends
Sleepy Time Baby Bear
Cats in Charge

Others
Expressive Tree People
Studies of Life – Poetry, Love Sonnets &
Thoughts

Questions - zjavanee@gmail.com